Very Bad Things

SUSAN MCBRIDE

Very Bad Things

DELACORTE PRESS

Text copyright © 2014 by Susan McBride
Jacket art copyright © 2014 by Dean Turpin

randomhouse.com/teens

Educators and librarians, for a variety of teaching tools, visit us at RHTeachersLibrarians.com

Library of Congress Cataloging-in-Publication Data
McBride, Susan.
Very bad things / Susan McBride. — First edition.
pages cm
Summary: "When a photo of Katie's popular boyfriend Mark having drunken sex with a tattooed girl at a party goes viral at their exclusive boarding school, Katie is devastated. Mark swears that he doesn't remember anything. But Rose, the girl in the photo, is missing—and Katie receives a gruesome present in the mail: a badly wrapped severed hand with a red rose tattoo"—Provided by publisher.
ISBN 978-0-385-73797-5 (hc : alk. paper) — ISBN 978-0-385-90704-0
(glb : alk. paper) — ISBN 978-0-385-37102-5 (ebook : alk. paper)
[1. Mystery and detective stories. 2. Murder—Fiction. 3. Boarding schools—Fiction.
4. Schools—Fiction.] I. Title.
PZ7.M478276Ve 2014
[Fic]—dc23
2013021675

The text of this book is set in 12-point Adobe Garamond.

Book design by Trish Parcell

Printed in the United States of America

10 9 8 7 6 5 4 3 2 1

First Edition

To Christina,

for all the pep talks while I wrote

(and rewrote) this book—

you're the best cheerleader ever!

SECRETS ARE GENERALLY TERRIBLE.

BEAUTY IS NOT HIDDEN—

ONLY UGLINESS AND DEFORMITY.

—*L. M. MONTGOMERY*

PROLOGUE

"I had the same dream again last night, the one where I wake up and someone's standing over me. I can feel him there. And I can hear him breathing. He says my name in this creepy whisper."

"*Him?* Could you see a face?" Dr. Capello asked, watching Katie from beneath a fringe of dark bangs.

"No," Katie said. "Only shadows."

Dr. Capello made a soft *hmm* sound. "Sometimes dreams about being watched mean we're feeling scrutinized or judged."

"I guess so." Katie shifted in her seat. She did worry a lot: about graduation, about her mom alone in St. Louis, about being with Mark. Maybe Mark most all. Not everyone was as happy as she was that they were together.

"Are you feeling threatened?"

She shrugged, though the question made her uneasy. "Not really."

The boarding school's consulting psychiatrist leaned forward, arms on her knees. "Is there anything else you remember about the dream? Any details?"

"Just that I can't move. I want to get up, but I'm paralyzed. I try to call out, but I have no voice. And then I smell it."

"What?" Dr. Capello's chair creaked.

"Roses," Katie said, and exhaled slowly. "It's always roses, and something else kind of rank. My heart's racing when I wake up, and I'm gasping for air, like I've been underwater too long."

"But no one's there, right? You take back control, reassuring yourself that it's only a nightmare."

"No one's there." Katie met Dr. Capello's eyes. "It's just me. But I have a hard time going back to sleep. I smell the roses even afterward, like it wasn't a dream at all. Like it was real."

CHAPTER ONE

KATIE

" 'The moon is distant from the sea, and yet with amber hands, she leads him, docile as a boy, along appointed sands. . . .' "

Katie Barton stopped. "C'mon, *think*," she told herself. She had to recite the Emily Dickinson poem for a lit class the next morning. It was almost midnight, and she was having a hard time staying awake. Her brain felt like mush. She wished she'd smuggled in some coffee, even if it was the rank stuff from the cafeteria. Trying hard to focus, she squinted at the sputtering light over the metal desk, buried in the midst of the library's upper stacks.

The stained-glass windows above the bookshelves had gone dark hours ago. The Whitney Prep library stayed open till midnight during midterms, and Katie was often the last one out the doors. She'd tried to study in her dorm, but she couldn't escape the noisy girls at Amelia House. Besides, she liked the quiet and the smell of dusty old books.

It's hopeless, she thought, and laid her head on her arms, closing her eyes. *Forget Emily Dickinson.*

Instead, she pictured the big grin on Mark's face when the hockey team had clinched a spot in the state championship. He'd grabbed her hard and kissed her right in front of all of Whitney. "I'm the king of the world!" he'd said, and laughed. Katie had gotten chills. She was almost afraid someone would pinch her and she'd realize she had imagined it. Everything about being with Mark felt too good to be true. When it was still pitch-dark this morning, he'd texted her to meet him behind her dorm. Despite the risk of getting caught, Katie had snuck out. They'd huddled together on the bench in the shadow of Amelia House, shivering as they'd held on to each other. For a few hours, they'd whispered and kissed until the sky was streaked with pink.

It was no wonder she was so tired. She could hardly keep her eyes open. . . .

Kay-tee.

Did someone say her name? The floor made the tiniest *creak, creak.*

"Mark?" she said groggily.

The soft tread on the old floors stopped. She heard quiet breaths behind her. Then something brushed her hair with the lightness of a moth. She jerked around in her chair, her heart thudding.

Katie blinked into the darkness, hearing hushed footsteps,

as if a mouse were scurrying across the wood. The bulb above the desk flickered and dimmed. She touched the pad of her laptop, waking up the screen to give herself more light, but her cozy niche in the stacks was still cloaked in shadows. She peered around, sure that someone else was there.

"Mrs. Ticknor?" she said. Only she didn't detect the librarian's telltale lavender perfume. She thought she smelled roses.

I'm so exhausted, I'm hallucinating, she told herself.

Or else she'd briefly dreamed that dream again, the one that always felt so real.

The hairs on her neck prickled. She reached down for her book bag, but instead of canvas, her fingertips touched something both silky soft and sharp enough to pierce her skin.

"Oh!" She drew her finger to her mouth, tasting blood.

Petals and thorns.

Her pulse thudded in her ears as she retrieved a rose from the floor. Its stem was freshly clipped, the petals damp. Suddenly, she was wide awake.

"Who's there?" she asked the shadows, heart slapping hard against her ribs. "Tessa?" She said her roommate's name. "Quit messing with me. It's not funny!"

Katie waited for laughter, but there was none.

She thought she saw something pale move in the dark, and she dropped the rose. She snatched up her things and shoved them into her bag. Pushing back her chair, she ran through the dimly lit aisles.

Halfway down the stairs, she bumped into Mrs. Ticknor. "Oh, good, Miss Barton!" The librarian's heavy perfume enveloped Katie in a lavender cloud. "I was just coming up to find you. The library's closing, and you're the last one here."

"No." Katie shook her head. "Someone else was in the stacks."

"That's not possible," Mrs. Ticknor said, and gave her a funny look. "It's just you and me—"

But Katie was already on her way out the door.

CHAPTER TWO

KATIE

ily k8e

The glow from her iPhone screen lit a spark in the dark as Katie read the message one more time. "I love you, too," she whispered, figuring she'd spoken too softly to be heard. But her roommate had bat ears.

"Oh, for Pete's sake," Tessa Lupinski grumbled from the other bed, and Katie let the screen go black. "Would you just call the guy and get it over with?"

"I can't." Katie sighed.

"Then go to sleep!" Tessa replied. "You should be counting sheep, not texting sappy love notes." She cleared her throat. "How do I love thee? Let me count the ways! Do I love thee more than a slap shot? Nay, a power-play goal, or a cross-check?"

"Stop." Katie tried not to laugh.

"Call. Him."

"No," Katie said, though she wanted to. "It's after one. He's probably gone to bed."

"Ha!" Tessa snorted. "You know he's still partying with the hockey jocks in the headmaster's house." Then she added in a singsong voice, "While the headmaster's away, his son's Neanderthal friends will play. Isn't that how it goes?"

"They're just pumped about going to state." Katie glanced at her phone again. "Mark's dad is in Chicago till tomorrow, and even the maid's off. The house is totally empty. It's not like they'll get busted."

"Really? I'm sure the rowing team thought the same thing when they partied in the boathouse last fall. I don't think getting stoned and taking out the boats bare-assed has ever been an approved activity in the Whitney rule book."

Someone had posted pictures online, and even the *Barnard Gazette* had gotten wind of it. The headmaster hadn't been any more pleased about that than the rowing team's angry parents.

Tessa snickered. "Not exactly what Ivy League schools want to discuss in admissions interviews."

Katie rolled her eyes. "No one's going to get Mark in trouble."

"You think he's too big to fail?"

"Way too big," Katie said, because it was true.

Mark Summers wasn't just the star center on the Whitney Prep hockey team—the keystone of the Soaring Eagles' athletic program—he was also the son of Dr. Gregory Summers, the headmaster of Whitney Preparatory Academy. Summers raised millions for the school, traveling across the country and abroad to visit blue-blooded alums. No one was going to mess with him or his son. So if anyone ratted out Mark about the hockey club drinking at the headmaster's house, it wouldn't be her boyfriend who would suffer. Mark could get away with murder at Whitney.

"I hate that," Tessa groaned, as if reading her mind.

"What?"

"That the rich are different. If *we* broke the rules, *we'd* be out on our butts."

"Which is why we're the last ones out of the library during exams," Katie said, thinking of the night during midterms two weeks ago when someone had left her a rose in the stacks. She'd never said anything to Tessa. She still wondered if her roommate had been screwing with her. She'd once told Tessa about her weird dream, and Tessa had given her a look and told her to lay off the Mountain Dew before bedtime. No, if Tessa had crept into the library with the rose, she would have fessed up already, making a crack about how fast Katie had fled the stacks. So Katie had convinced herself that Mark had bribed a freshman to bring her the flower. When they'd first gotten together, he'd given her a rose, cutting it off the rose-bush himself. Maybe he just wanted to remind her of that. She wanted to believe it was that.

"Do you ever feel like Mark hooked up with you because you're everything he's not?" Tessa said out of the blue. "I mean, he's had his whole life handed to him on a silver platter, and he was dating that bitch Joelle Needham before you. What if he thought it'd be fun to go slumming?"

"Thanks for that," Katie muttered. It was annoying how Tessa always went back to the same place.

"You know what I mean."

Yeah, she knew, because she'd had her own doubts about Mark at first. But she didn't anymore. She hated that Tessa wouldn't let her forget how insecure she'd been.

Katie lay still, biting her lip to keep from saying something she'd regret. She knew that her relationship with Mark made Tessa feel left out. Before Mark, she and Tessa had been inseparable. But it had been different these past few months since Katie and Mark had gotten together. Katie couldn't hide the fact that she'd rather be with Mark than anyone else. It was no wonder that Tessa felt hurt.

She chose her words carefully. "No one's forcing Mark to be with me. If I wasn't what he wanted, I couldn't stop him from dumping me like he dropped Joelle when she cheated on him."

"You can sound all casual about it," Tessa said through the dark, "but if he broke up with you, you'd die and you know it."

Katie wanted to deny it, but Tessa was right.

Mark *was* special. He was the guy all the girls drooled over and all the guys wanted to be. Which is why Katie had been stunned to see him standing in the back of the room at a poetry slam she'd helped organize in January. She remembered his eyes on her when she'd gotten up to read; how her hands had sweated so much that when she'd passed the microphone to Bea Lively, Bea had wiped it on her jeans. Afterward, Mark had hung around, asking if she wanted to grab coffee at the student center. Katie had babbled like an idiot the whole time. But Mark didn't seem to mind. They actually had a lot in common. They'd both lost a parent—Katie's dad had died when she was twelve and Mark's mom had walked out when he was a little kid. They'd met up again for coffee after that and then for a late-night showing of *Psycho* in the school auditorium, where he'd first put his arm around her. Katie had tried to keep it from Tessa, knowing she'd doubt Mark's motives. But it was hard to keep anything from her roommate. "All guys like him want is sex," Tessa had said the minute she found out.

"That's not true," Katie had defended him, because she didn't believe it. Mark didn't pressure her. He was actually really romantic. He sent her sweet texts just to say "i miss u." They took walks in the woods, holding hands and talking about everything under the sun. He'd even snuck her into the school's ice rink after hours. He'd helped her lace up her skates and held her up while she slipped and slid across the ice, giggling all the while.

Just last month, they were in the media room of the headmaster's house, watching a movie on the wide-screen. Mark had brought out a silver flask. "This is what fifty-year-old whiskey tastes like," he'd said, laughing when Katie had taken her first sip and winced. They'd passed it back and forth for a while (well, Katie had mostly passed it *back*); then Mark had looked her in the eye and asked, "Do you trust me?" When she'd answered, "Yes," he'd retrieved a flashlight and taken her hand, leading her into the unfinished part of the basement where there was a door marked MACHINE ROOM—DO NOT ENTER. Inside, it was filled with dusty old water tanks and an ancient boiler. "Follow me," Mark had said, going around the boiler and pushing aside an old grate. Then he'd ducked through a hole in the wall. "C'mon," he'd said, extending his hand to her. "I'll take care of you."

Katie wasn't sure what she was doing. Her heart was beating so wildly she couldn't think straight. She hadn't sipped enough whiskey to be drunk, but she felt amped up and giddy. Wasn't just being with Mark taking a risk? Every time she was with him, she fell harder. Who could say he wouldn't break her heart? She'd been so buttoned-up since she'd come to Whitney, so afraid of letting herself actually *feel* anything since her dad had passed away. Maybe it was time she took a bigger leap of faith.

"Okay," she said, and took his hand, bending down to enter the hole after him. Her feet stumbled over loose mortar, and she breathed in air that smelled stale, like it had been cut off from the outside for a very long time. "What is this place?"

"It's a secret," Mark said, drawing her along with him. The beam from the flashlight guided them as they slipped through the old steam tunnels that connected the buildings beneath the campus. "I used to hide down here a lot." He showed her a storage room cluttered with chalkboards, rolls of yellowed paper, textbooks, and wooden desks from another century. "I was eight when my dad took over at Whitney, after my mom left us. She cheated on him with a student at the college where he was dean," Mark had admitted. His voice was a little slurred from the whiskey but not enough to hide the bitterness. "There were times when he'd drink too much and get angry."

"Did he ever hurt you?" Katie had asked.

Mark had shrugged. "He'd scream and punch holes in the walls, that kind of thing. Now he's just sad. He still misses her, even after everything."

"I shut down after my dad died when I was twelve. It hurt so bad that I didn't want to feel anything at all," Katie had said before she could stop herself. Mark's confession had struck a chord, and she felt even more connected. "It was like he'd walked out on us, and I guess that's what he did. He just bailed instead of sticking around to deal with the bad stuff, like we would've loved him less because he'd screwed up."

"I'm sorry." Mark had sighed and held her hand more tightly. "That sucks."

"Yeah, it does."

For a long moment, they'd stood there, fingers entwined, saying nothing.

Then Mark had cleared his throat. "C'mon, let's go."

Before Katie knew it, he'd taken her deeper and deeper into the tunnels. Some places were so tight they practically had to crawl on hands and knees. But in the end, where he'd led her was worth it.

He shut off the flashlight and pushed open a grate above

them. He helped Katie up through it before climbing after her into the very warm room dappled with moonbeams. The air was heavy with the earthy scent of moss and flowers.

"Are we on another planet?" she joked.

"Almost. We're in the greenhouse." Mark drew her deep into the rows of plants, leaves brushing her face as they walked, until they were surrounded by blooming rosebushes. It was like finding paradise at the tail end of winter.

"Do you bring all your girlfriends here?" Katie said, only half teasing.

"No, you're the first," he admitted, and he took out his penknife to cut off a rose. He even pared off the thorns before he brushed the soft petals against her cheek, then tucked the flower behind her ear.

Katie had never had anyone do anything so sweet and romantic. She'd grabbed him and kissed him like she'd never kissed anyone before. He'd tasted like whiskey and warmth, and her heart had pounded so hard she'd thought her chest would explode. What happened between them that night had bound them so tightly that Katie was sure nothing could ever pull them apart. No matter what anyone said about Mark—that he was cocky and wasn't serious about anything but hockey, that he was using her—Katie trusted him.

"Enjoy it while it lasts," Joelle Needham had remarked after the hockey team's big win, when everyone was slapping Mark on the back and high-fiving him.

But Joelle was wrong, and Tessa, too.

What Katie had with Mark was real. She felt it in her bones.

Sighing, she clutched her iPhone and turned over in bed. She could hear Tessa's rhythmic breathing but sensed that she wasn't asleep. "No one understands him like I do," she said. "He's different when he's with me."

"Just because you convince yourself something's true doesn't mean it is," Tessa replied, and Katie hated that her best friend didn't understand.

"You're jealous."

"Jealous? Please!" Tessa's bedsprings creaked. "You might see Prince Charming, but all I see is a frog. Now would you put your phone down and go to sleep?"

But Katie had a hard time falling asleep. It felt like hours before she finally drifted off. When she did, she dreamed again of someone standing beside her bed, watching her, and she breathed in the smell of damp earth and roses. She struggled to wake up, gasping as she finally surfaced. She opened her eyes, panicked.

"Tessa?" she called out, and looked across the room for the familiar lump beneath the covers.

Only Tessa's bed was empty.

CHAPTER THREE

MARK

Boom ba ba boom ba ba boom.

The music throbbed inside Mark Summers's head, the bass pulsing through his chest and banging his rib cage like a heavy-metal heartbeat.

Someone had turned off the lights in the basement rec room and switched on a lava lamp, spilling clouds of red and blue across the walls. Steve Getty had snuck in a couple of townies eager to impress Whitney Prep's hockey club. Though, at the moment, only one girl was in sight. The other had disappeared on her way to the john. She'd been gone so long that Mark wondered if she was stealing something. The girl left behind was in the midst of a sad striptease, shedding all but her bra and panties. She moved sloppily from one drunken guy to another, doing her best imitation of a lap dance.

When she tripped over Mark, he got up and moved out of reach despite her slurred "Hey, where ya goin'?" and the protests of his friends. But he felt sick watching her pathetic bumps and grinds, and not just because his mind was on Katie.

The colored lights pulsing and swirling made him dizzy, and he blinked to clear his eyes. Only that didn't work. With every second, the fog in his brain thickened, his stomach churned.

He hadn't drunk that much, had he?

He headed toward the stairs, holding a cup with one hand and grabbing the banister with the other. Once he'd made it to the first floor's rear hallway, he had to lean against the wall, squeezing his eyes shut.

What the hell was going on? He'd just had one beer and started on his second, which Steve had tapped from the keg not ten minutes ago. Mark had promised Katie that he wouldn't get wasted. He'd only half emptied the cup in his hand. He should barely be buzzed.

But something was wrong. He was practically drooling, and his head felt hazy. Numbness seeped through him so that he staggered when he walked. Bumping into a table, he set crystal to rattling. He fought to steady himself before he knocked anything over and broke it.

Be careful, Mark! Those are priceless antiques! He could hear his father ranting. *They belong to Whitney, not to me!*

Yeah, he thought, rubbing his eyes, *just like everything else around here.*

"You okay, man?" someone said. A hand gripped his shoulder.

"Yeah . . . no . . . I don't know," he mumbled, squinting as he focused hard on the familiar face with its crooked nose and worried frown. "Charlie." He mouthed the name of his goalie and best friend.

Maybe having the guys over while his dad was out of town wasn't such a great idea. Maybe he should tell everyone to clear out so he could go lie down. Was he getting the flu?

"Want me to tell Steve to take the girls home?" Charlie Frazer asked, as if reading his thoughts.

But Mark wasn't listening.

I'm gonna puke, he realized as his stomach lurched, and he dropped his drink. The cup hit his shoe, splashing beer across the polished floor.

"Summers?" Charlie sounded worried.

He jerked away. "I need air," he said, fighting the dizziness. He staggered down the hallway toward the back door. He had to get out of the house, had to stop the lights from swirling and his head from spinning, or he'd spew all over the expensive Persian rugs. But he didn't make it outside.

Halfway there, he tripped and fell to his knees. For a moment, he stayed on all fours, his balance so off that he couldn't get up on his own.

What was wrong with him?

"Are you okay?" a soft voice asked, and a hand reached

down for his arm. "Here, hang on to me." The girl grabbed his hand, helping him struggle to his feet.

He sucked in a whiff of her perfume, so sweet it made him gag.

"You should lie down for a sec."

Mark squinted through his haze, trying hard to focus on her face: dark hair, dark eyes. He blinked. "Katie?" he said, slurring the two syllables.

"C'mon, you look like hell." Her arm went around him.

Mark's legs felt like jelly.

Moaning pathetically, he allowed himself to be led into the small room tucked behind the kitchen. He could hardly keep his eyes open, couldn't form the words to speak. He needed to crash, couldn't keep going.

"Relax," the soft voice instructed.

She pushed him down, and Mark fell onto the bed.

A tiny bit of light glowed from the corner like the screen on a cell phone. Was someone else there? He saw the crucifix hung on the wall. This was the maid's room. But Annalisa was off. Why was he here?

He tried to lift his head but couldn't. His muscles didn't work. All he could do was lie back and breathe. The sticky-sweet perfume filled his nose again. It wasn't Katie. She smelled nothing like Katie.

He moaned as the weight of her body settled on his legs, pressing him into the mattress. Hands slipped beneath his shirt, sliding up his chest and playing with the St. Sebastian medal that Katie had given him before the play-offs began.

It was supposed to protect him. Cool air made goose bumps race across his skin as his shirt came off. But he was so out of it, he couldn't lift a finger to stop her.

"Don't fight it. We'll be done before you know it," she said, her lips touching his jaw and then his mouth.

Mark wanted to push her off. But he couldn't. He was too far gone already.

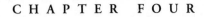

CHAPTER FOUR

TESSA

Tessa frowned, gazing out the bus window at Katie and Mark Summers. If Katie didn't hurry up and board, she was going to miss the delightful trip to the morgue with their AP Biology class. Then again, Katie probably wouldn't care. All she thought about these days was *Mark, Mark, Mark.* It made Tessa want to gag.

Despite it being a gloomy Monday morning, Mark wore a baseball cap and shades. She bet he still had a monster hangover. He'd been too out of it to see Katie on Sunday, which had suited Tessa perfectly. Although it had Katie so anxious that she spent the entire day endlessly checking her phone.

Tessa squinted at Mark. "You're not as special as you think," she whispered.

Something was definitely up. Prince Charming wasn't his clean-cut self today. The tail of his shirt hung out beneath his blazer, and his rumpled pants looked like he'd slept in them. But Katie hardly seemed repelled. As usual, she'd dumped Tessa the moment she'd seen Mark sitting on the steps of the administration building, waiting for her. Now she couldn't stop touching him. Her fingers were on his face, on his arms, on the back of his neck.

Ugh.

"Aw, check out the lovebirds! They're so into each other they wouldn't notice if the bus blew up. Makes you want to hurl, doesn't it?"

Tessa hadn't realized that Steve Getty had slid in beside her until he'd opened his big, fat mouth. Even if she agreed with him, she wasn't about to show it.

"That's Katie's spot."

"Is it?"

She glared at him.

He shrugged and rubbed a hand over eyes bagged with shadows. He had tiny scratches on his chin and neck, like he'd shaved in the dark. "If she's lucky, the bus will take off without her, and she'll miss this lame trip entirely. You're probably looking forward to it, huh? You're paler than any corpse they could show us." Steve squinted at her. "Can you talk to dead people?"

"Get out of Katie's seat," Tessa tried again, refusing to rise to the bait. She would not lose it in front of Steve Getty. She wouldn't give him the satisfaction. He seemed to think he could be as obnoxious as he wanted just because his dad was an ambassador from some tiny country whose claim to fame was gambling and offshore banks.

"Katie's not here." He leaned toward her, putting his arms around her to point out the window. "If you haven't noticed, she's busy sucking face with Summers. Though my boy's not looking too good after the weekend, is he? I'll bet he's been popping aspirin like Tic Tacs."

"Good." Tessa pushed him off her. "Now go away."

"What? Do I reek?" Steve sniffed the armpits of his burgundy blazer. "Or are you just not that into guys? I have heard rumors about you. Lots of rumors—"

"And *I* heard that Whitney's the fifth boarding school your dad's shipped you off to," Tessa snapped. "Is it because you're such an ass that no one can stand you for more than a semester?"

"You know, Lupinski," he said, and she felt his hot breath on her cheek, "I'll bet you'd be almost pretty if I was wasted and you loosened up. I'd even go so far as to say you'd be a ball of fire." He put his hand on her thigh and squeezed.

"You're such a douche!" Tessa tried to shove his hand away, but it wouldn't budge. "Let go or I'll scream."

His chiseled features turned hard as he released her. "For someone who likes to play with fire, you're totally frigid, you know?" He rubbed his arms and made a *brrr* noise. "Lucky for Summers your roommate's not so uptight. He had one hell of a weekend."

"What's that supposed to mean?" Tessa asked, tugging her skirt firmly over her knees.

Steve grinned, but the smile didn't reach his eyes. "Guess that's for me to know and you to find out."

"What are you, four?"

"Are we talking dog years?" he asked, unbuttoning his blazer as he stood. His broad shoulders blotted out any light down the aisle.

"I think you've had one too many pucks to the head," Tessa muttered, relieved when he walked to the back of the bus to join his friends.

The bus vibrated as the driver cranked the engine, and Tessa looked out the window to see Mark walking away, hands in his pockets, head hanging. At least he wasn't going on their field trip this morning, so Tessa wouldn't have to tolerate him for Katie's sake. Having one hockey thug like Steve Getty along was bad enough.

"Phew!" Katie said, scooting in beside her.

Two seconds later, the bus lurched away from the curb.

"That was close," Tessa remarked, not wanting to sound pissed even if she was a little. "I was afraid you'd get left behind."

"I wouldn't bail on you," Katie said, and slid her book bag under the seat.

"Not even for Romeo?"

"He's got things to do."

"Like explain to Daddy why the house smells like a brewery?" Tessa asked.

"He has to find something that's missing," Katie said, staring out the window.

Tessa changed the subject. "You okay? You're not worried about seeing a dead guy, are you? Promise you won't heave like you did when we had to dissect a baby pig."

"I'm seriously praying I don't lose it." Katie reached for Tessa's hand. "But I'm not worried about me. I'm worried about *you*. Are you cool with going to the morgue? It's right across from the cemetery. I know you try to hide it, but it has to eat at you, what with your whole family buried there and—"

"I'm fine." Tessa didn't let Katie finish. "I'm over it. That was a long time ago," she added, tucking pale hair behind her ears. But Katie's brown eyes got soft, and it was clear that her friend didn't believe her. "I'm all right. Really," Tessa insisted.

Still, Katie gave her hand a squeeze.

Tessa pulled her hand from Katie's and gazed down at her lap. She'd lied when she'd said it didn't bother her to see the cemetery. It bothered her a lot.

It had been ten years since the fire had reduced her family to tombstones in the Barnard Township Cemetery: one marker each for her parents and her older brother, Peter. Tessa did try really hard not to think about it. But no matter how often she told herself she couldn't change what had happened that night, a part of her felt guilty and always would.

It didn't help that everyone at Whitney knew about her past, or at least knew the gossip. Sometimes she wished she could tell them the whole truth instead of leaving it buried. But Tessa couldn't set things straight. It was impossible. So she'd gotten used to the whispers. Those she could tolerate. But when someone made jokes about it, like Steve Getty's "playing with fire" crack, that was harder to swallow.

He'll get what's coming, she told herself. Guys like him could weasel out of trouble only so many times.

Besides, people like Steve Getty didn't matter. She didn't need everyone to like her. Katie was the only friend she needed, the only one who'd never judged her. Katie didn't listen to the rumors. And that was why Tessa would be there for Katie when she finally saw Mark Summers for who he really was. When he broke her friend's heart for good, Tessa would be the one who helped her pick up the pieces.

CHAPTER FIVE

KATIE

The body lay naked in the center of the room.

Beneath the harsh lights, the skin appeared yellow and waxen. The small group of AP Biology students stood in a loose circle around it. They all wore latex gloves and plastic aprons that crackled when they moved. A strained silence made every breath and anxious cough seem twice as loud.

"Ladies and gentleman, I'd like you to meet Mr. Thaddeus Ogden, who very kindly donated his body and his organs to Barnard Hospital's cadaver lab so that young minds like yours might consider careers in the medical field," Dr. Albert Arnold said, standing in front of the gurney. He gently patted Mr. Ogden's lifeless shoulder. "The Whitney sisters' foundation supports much of the research we do, and a good number of doctors and scientists, myself included, are Whitney alums. Most began their path to medicine right here where you are now, with the same hands-on experience."

"He doesn't look real, does he?" Tessa whispered in Katie's ear. "The body, I mean, not Dr. Arnold."

"Real enough," Katie whispered back. As she'd predicted, she felt like throwing up.

She couldn't stand the smell of formaldehyde. The stuff out-and-out reeked and, once it got into your nose, it was there to stay. You could pop a can of cheese Pringles and breathe it in after spending an hour poking open the insides of a pickled frog—or a mouse or a piglet—but the stink wouldn't go away. And this time, they weren't dissecting a pint-sized critter or even a medium-sized one, which was bad enough. This morning, their corpse du jour was big and entirely human.

"Blech." The noise inadvertently escaped her.

"If you're gonna hurl, don't do it on my kicks," Steve Getty said, loudly enough for the whole room to hear. He made a show of stepping farther away from her, garnering snickers from his buddies.

"Maybe I'll aim for them," she replied.

"My dear, there's no need to be squeamish," Dr. Arnold said, looking directly at her. "Mr. Ogden's a very willing volunteer. He's not going to sit up and say 'Ouch.'"

"That's reassuring," Katie murmured, hoping the image of a dead Mr. Ogden popping upright wouldn't stick in her head.

It wasn't that she was afraid of slicing through skin and finding guts and bones. It was touching something dead that had been alive, that had once felt things, maybe even loved or at least been hungry and sleepy and *breathing*. Worse still, the corpse on the slab looked a lot like her granddad, who'd died the year before her father. Her dad's casket had been closed and covered with a spray of roses. But her granddad's had been open. So the last time she saw him was at the visitation. Afterward, she wished she'd just remembered him as he was: alive and happy, not made up and dressed up, with bloodless hands folded neatly on his chest.

Don't look at his face, she told herself. *Anywhere but the face.* Or else she would be reminded that Mr. Ogden wasn't made of wax but skin and bones.

"So," Dr. Arnold asked eagerly, looking at the students around him, "which one of you wants to take the first stab?"

Katie focused on the doctor instead of the dead man. He was seriously working the mad-scientist thing, she thought, with his bulging eyes and tufts of gray hair and the way he poked at the air with the thin blade clutched in his latex-gloved hand. She'd heard that he used to be Barnard's medical examiner before he took over the cadaver lab. She imagined him walking around the morgue at night, chatting with the corpses. *Well, hello, Mrs. Smith. Not too cold in there, are you?*

She must've made a funny noise, as Tessa gave her a weird look.

"You okay?" her roommate whispered.

Katie nodded, though she felt anything but.

"Hey, I think Katie's volunteering," Steve Getty said loudly, then leaned over to hiss, "Or are you chicken? *Baawk baawk.*"

"Bite me," she murmured, feeling Dr. Arnold's overly bright gaze lock on her like a guided missile.

"Young lady, are you up to the challenge? As I said before, you won't hurt him. Mr. Ogden possesses a superhumanly high pain threshold," the lab director quipped, raising tangled eyebrows as he extended the scalpel. "I'll even make it easy on you. Would you like to cut our cadaver's flexor tendons so we can examine his ulnar artery? It's as good a place to start as any."

"Me?" Katie's hands were sweating in her latex gloves. She rubbed them down the front of the surgical apron they'd all been made to wear. She had her hair tucked up in a scrub cap, and her scalp was starting to itch. "No, thanks. I'm sure there's someone else who'd like to go first."

She glanced hopefully at the other faces in the circle, but no one seemed eager to step forward.

Dr. Arnold wasn't about to let her off the hook. "Don't you want to play *CSI*? I thought everyone did."

"I'm pretty sure they don't use real bodies on TV," Katie replied.

"Aw, c'mon, don't be a wuss," Steve Getty said, and Katie felt his meaty paw on her back, propelling her forward. She stumbled toward Dr. Arnold, who caught her arm, stopping her forward motion before she ended up flinging herself across Mr. Ogden on the slab.

"Now, now, no need to shove," Dr. Arnold said.

Katie gave Steve a nasty look. Then she glanced helplessly at Tessa, who looked so mad she'd turned purple.

"Well, my dear, why don't you go ahead and kick things off since you're up here." The doctor passed her the scalpel. "Just take a deep breath, relax, and approach it clinically. Go on." He put a hand on her shoulder, turning her toward the corpse.

A deep breath was the last thing Katie needed. The formaldehyde stink was already making her dizzy.

As the circle of classmates closed in on her, Katie swallowed and took a step nearer Mr. Ogden. *You can do this,* she told herself, holding the thin blade in her hand as she lowered it to the dead man's wrist. Behind her back, Steve made clucking noises. Katie tried to ignore him, though she felt the weight of everyone's eyes. Her hands began to sweat inside her gloves.

"I've clearly marked the area over the tendon," Dr. Arnold was saying. "Once you're done, I'll do some pinning and then we'll give everyone a chance to look." His voice buzzed in her ears like a hive of bees.

Katie stared at the blue marks on the skin at the cadaver's wrist, trying hard not to glance at the face with its sunken cheeks and eyes closed in a forever kind of sleep.

Were you married, Mr. Ogden? Did you like your job? Did you die alone, or with someone holding your hand?

She pursed her lips, pressing down on the scalpel, denting the skin but not piercing it. Corpses didn't bleed, right? But what if he did sit up? she thought. She'd heard of it happening before. What was it called? Rigor mortis? No, that wasn't it. Involuntary muscle contraction?

"She doesn't want to do it, for God's sake!" Tessa's voice rang out, followed by the *clop-clop* of her footsteps. Then she nudged Katie aside and took the surgical blade from her trembling fingers.

"Miss Lupinski?" Dr. Arnold asked, squinting at Tessa. "Are you certain *you're* up to the task?"

"Yes," Tessa said simply, and, without hesitation, she sliced firmly into Mr. Ogden, following the perpendicular lines that Dr. Arnold had mapped out. Within minutes, she had the flaps pinned back so all the tendons and veins and the artery were visible.

Déjà vu, Katie thought as she stood there and watched. It was like freshman biology all over again, when she'd wimped out and Tessa had taken charge of their first frog, slicing it open with the same decisiveness.

When Tessa was done, she stepped away from the corpse, saying nothing. She quietly returned the scalpel to the lab director before stepping back into her place in the circle to Katie's left.

"Bravo, my dear. Well done," Dr. Arnold cheered.

Steve let out a low whistle. "That is one stone-cold bitch," he murmured from Katie's right, just loud enough for her to hear.

CHAPTER SIX

KATIE

"Thanks for the save," Katie said to Tessa once they were on the bus, heading back to Whitney. "I should've stabbed Steve with the scalpel while I had the chance."

"He probably would've enjoyed it," Tessa said. "He's a hockey player. They're like vampires. They get off on blood."

"He's been giving me a hard time since Mark and I got together. He'd love to break us up, just to mess with Mark's head. Steve hates that Mark is captain *and* a power forward," Katie said, because it was the truth. "He wants Mark out so he can be the star, but it's not going to happen."

Tessa pulled out her phone and stared at the screen like her life depended on it.

If you can't say something nice, don't say anything at all, huh? Katie thought. Okay, so maybe Steve Getty wasn't the only one who wished she and Mark would split up. He could stand in line behind Joelle Needham and Tessa.

Whatever.

Katie turned away from her friend and gazed out at the scenery, grabbing hold of the seat in front of her as the bus hit a bump in the road. The country lane that connected the quaint town of Barnard with the private grounds of Whitney Prep was a mixture of potholes and gravel. If you didn't know better, you wouldn't have a clue that such an unassuming path led to hundreds of acres of landscaped grounds full of ivy and roses, encircled by towering pines. On sunny days, Katie thought the campus looked picture perfect, like something you'd see on a postcard. When it was gloomy, she found the historic brick and stone buildings pretty creepy, with their Gothic arches and murky stained-glass windows.

Whitney wasn't exactly home, but Katie had adapted well enough these past four years. Whenever she got homesick, she'd remind herself that her father had once arrived at the imposing wrought-iron gates as a scholarship kid, just like her. She doubted the school had changed much since then.

It was a twist of fate that eventually landed her at Whitney Prep. Her dad had always wanted her to go, but her mom had been dead set against sending her so far away. "No eleven-year-old girl should be apart from her mother," Katie remembered hearing her mother argue. "Besides, she's been attending St. Mary's since preschool. It'd break her heart to leave her friends there."

That was back when Katie's dad was alive and they'd lived in a big house in a posh suburb, when her mom had dabbled in the Junior League and played tennis at the country club.

But that life had disappeared when Katie turned twelve, the market crashed, and her dad lost everything. He'd died in their garage, sitting in his Mercedes sedan with the engine running. "Heart attack," her mom told everyone, but Katie knew no one believed her. When the dust had settled, they had next to nothing. Her mom went to work as a secretary so they could afford to rent an apartment, and Katie transferred to public school. Katie missed her friends at St. Mary's. She felt like an outcast at public school, especially since everyone gossiped about her behind her back. She wasn't just the new girl. She was "the girl whose dad had offed himself."

After her dad had been buried and the lawyers had sorted through the mess of paperwork, they found something that had stunned both Katie and her mother: before he'd killed himself, her dad had sent off an application for Katie to go to Whitney on scholarship. And she'd been accepted.

Instead of freaking out and insisting Katie stay home, her mom had seemed relieved. "I hate that you're going away, sweetheart," she'd said, "but your dad was right. Whitney's as good an education as you'll get anywhere, and it's what he always wanted."

Losing her dad had been rough all around. Her mom hardly acted like her mother anymore. Katie figured it was the Valium that her mom swallowed like aspirin. It made her numb, like a walking zombie. She could barely take care of herself, much less Katie.

So Katie's bags had been packed, and she'd been shipped off to Whitney to start her freshman year.

She'd met Tessa right off the bat, when they were thrown together in Amelia House, one of the girls' dorms. "You're a scholly kid, too, huh?" Tessa had remarked before even saying hello. "They like sticking us charity cases together."

Katie remembered being struck by Tessa's ice-blue eyes and her tough-girl demeanor. It had taken a while for Tessa to trust her. Now Katie wondered if she was the only person in the world Tessa trusted.

She pressed her forehead to the window splashed with drizzle as the rain began to fall, and her thoughts turned to Mark. She was happy he'd been hanging around to see her off on the bus this morning, but he'd looked so tired and anxious. When she'd asked what was up, he'd grumbled about trying to find something that was missing.

"Do you need me to help?"

"Nope."

"Did you lose it at the party?"

"Not sure."

What kind of answer was that?

"How wasted were you?" Katie asked.

"I wasn't wasted!" he'd snapped. "Two beers don't get me drunk."

"Okay, okay." She'd backed off, not used to him barking at her like that.

"Sorry." He'd pressed his mouth into a tight line, and Katie had known there was something he wasn't telling her.

She'd touched his cheek. "You can talk to me, you know."

"I know." He had sighed. "Okay, don't hate me, but I can't find the St. Sebastian medal."

"You lost it? Oh, Mark." Katie had given it to him right before the prep school hockey play-offs. St. Sebastian looked after athletes and soldiers, which felt like one and the same whenever Katie watched Mark on the ice. And he had the biggest game yet of the season two weeks off. "I can skip the trip to the morgue and help you look for it."

"No," Mark had replied, and rubbed his stubbly jaw. "I'll find it. I'm just having some trouble remembering stuff."

Katie had squinted at him. "But you said you weren't drunk."

"I *wasn't*." He'd glanced around them and tugged down the bill of his cap. "Can we not talk about this? I feel like crap, and I need to get to class."

"Sure." Katie didn't want to argue. Instead, she'd forced a smile and kept it light. "I'll see you when I'm back from dissecting a dead guy, okay?"

He'd tousled her hair. "Yeah, have fun with that."

She had paused on the bus's steps and glanced back at Mark as he'd walked away, feeling a knot in the pit of her stomach. She felt that knot even now as she stared out the window at a uniformed guard waving the bus onto campus. Katie peered through the drizzle as the administration building came into view.

There was Mark, his arms crossed as he leaned against a pillar. He put a hand above his eyes, and Katie knew he was looking for her. She beat on the window until he spotted her and waved back.

Tessa groaned. "Ever heard of playing hard to get?"

"Why? He's already got me," Katie said. She couldn't stand

up fast enough when the bus finally parked. It let out a gassy puff and then a squeal as the pleated door opened. Chatter swelled around them as Katie stood, nudging Tessa into the aisle.

"So do you want to grab lunch?" Tessa said as they disembarked. "It's spaghetti today, isn't it?"

"Yeah, I guess," Katie murmured, only half listening.

"Hey!" She heard Mark's voice above the others and then saw his blond hair and wide shoulders pushing through the crush of people as he made his way toward her.

"Hey, yourself!" Katie said, and dropped her bag to throw her arms around him, holding on tight. The Whitney rule book stated: *No public displays of affection on campus shall be tolerated.* Right. Maybe that made sense to the Whitney sisters who'd founded the school a hundred fifty years ago. Katie had seen old paintings of them. Calling them ugly was an understatement. She highly doubted they'd had to worry about PDAs with anyone. But how was she supposed to resist a guy who smelled as good as Mark? She inhaled the sweetness of his skin, like soap and citrus and something entirely masculine.

"You must've missed me," he said, and drew back, resting his forehead on hers.

"I did." Katie's heart swelled. She was happy to see him looking more like himself. "I hope everything lost is found?"

"I've got the most important thing right here," he said, sidestepping her question by distracting her with a kiss.

Tessa cleared her throat. "If you haven't noticed, our bug-eyed AP Bio instructor, Mr. Archibald, is staring daggers over here. So unless you're itching for demerits, you should put a little space between you."

Katie sighed. "C'mon, Tessa—"

"She's right." Mark leaned closer to whisper, "I don't want to get you in trouble."

Reluctantly, she took a step back and turned to see that Mr. Archibald was indeed watching. She gave him a little wave, which softened his pinched expression the tiniest bit.

Katie turned back to her boyfriend.

"You up for lunch?" she asked, and Mark nodded. "Good, 'cause Tessa and I were headed that way, weren't we?"

Her roommate uttered an unenthusiastic "Uh-huh."

Mark grabbed Katie's bag and slung it over his shoulder. She caught his hand and laced her fingers with his. "I don't want to see another corpse as long as I live," she told him as they walked. "Poor Mr. Ogden. He looked so—"

"Dead?" Tessa finished for her.

Katie stuck her tongue out at her friend.

"So it went okay?" Mark asked. "I can't picture you cutting up a worm, much less a person."

"Well." Katie paused, making a face. "I didn't exactly, um, I kind of couldn't go through with it."

"Katie's a marshmallow." Tessa caught up with them, her long legs keeping pace. "She's not good with blood and guts."

"Tessa came to my rescue," Katie admitted.

Mark wrinkled his brow. "What happened?"

"You should ask your buddy Steve," Tessa said, her head down.

"What about Steve?" Mark stopped just outside the cafeteria. He caught Katie by the arm. "Did he do something to you?"

"It doesn't matter." Katie tugged at his hand. "He's not worth worrying about."

"It matters to me," Mark insisted. He looked at Tessa. "What?"

"Tessa, don't," Katie said under her breath, but Tessa ignored her.

"The jerk shoved your girlfriend into the dead guy's lap, that's what," Tessa reported, stretching the truth by a hair. "Now can we go inside and have some spaghetti like everyone else?" Tessa waved at the students coming and going around them. "Or should we stand here and take a poll on whether or not Steve Getty is the biggest douche on the planet?"

CHAPTER SEVEN

KATIE

Voices swirled around them the moment they stepped inside the dining hall. Heads turned as they walked past. Katie felt like everyone in the room was watching them and whispering. Mark didn't seem to notice, but then he was used to being the center of attention. It made Katie uneasy.

Had the whole school already heard about her panic attack at the morgue?

She stared down at her feet, hanging on to Mark's hand as he headed toward the lunch line.

"Hey, bro! Over here!" A whoop rose from a table filled with Mark's teammates, and Katie caught Steve Getty waving wildly at them.

To her dismay, Mark let go of her hand and walked straight in Steve's direction.

Katie glared at Tessa. "Look what you started," she said, and went after him.

"Summers, you dog!" Steve smirked as Mark approached. He stepped over the bench and gave Mark a slap on the back. "I might've expected it from you, but not her," he added, eyebrows arching as Katie approached. "Guess she just pretends to be shy, huh?"

"What the hell are you talking about?" Mark asked, shaking off Steve's arm. He dropped Katie's book bag. "You can stir shit with me all you want, but leave Katie out of it."

"Mark?" Katie stepped between them. "Let's go get lunch."

"Yeah, don't mind me." Steve threw his hands up, backing off. "Just thought I'd give you a heads-up about the picture going viral, that's all."

"What picture?" Katie asked, and she glanced at Charlie, Mark's best friend on the hockey squad. Though he sat at the table next to Steve, he didn't even look up. "What's going on?"

"Getty must be bored with sending pics of his hairy ass to everyone." Mark snatched up her book bag and grabbed her hand. "Sounds like he's playing cut and paste with Photoshop."

"It's your funeral!" Steve called after them.

Katie glanced back over her shoulder to see Steve grinning—but there was something else in his face. Something raw and angry. "He's not exactly your biggest fan, is he?"

"The feeling's mutual," Mark said.

Katie saw Charlie get up, like he wanted to come after Mark, but Steve clamped a hand on his shoulder and he settled back into his seat.

"Aren't you curious?" Katie asked as they got in line and Mark handed her a tray. "Don't you want to see for yourself?"

"Nah." Mark shrugged. "Knowing Steve, he's stuck my head on some porno dude's body. I'd kind of like to eat my lunch, not lose it."

Katie couldn't let it go. "What if it's not that at all? What if he's got a shot of you drinking? That could keep you from playing in the state championship, maybe even bar you from graduation, no matter who your dad is," Katie said, her mind whirring. She wouldn't put anything past Steve Getty. Ever since he'd shown up at Whitney in the middle of last semester, he'd needed to be the star. Except Mark had that covered.

"Relax. I'm sure it's nothing," Mark insisted, sounding agitated. He slapped a plate of spaghetti on his tray, then headed to the nearest table, dropping their book bags on the floor.

Maybe he didn't notice people staring at them, but Katie did. And this time, she could tell that it wasn't because Mark stood out in a crowd. Something was clearly up, and Steve Getty was behind it.

"Why's everyone acting weird?" Tessa asked as she joined them at the table. "Do I have toilet paper stuck to my shoes? Is my skirt tucked into my underwear?"

"It's not you," Katie said.

Tessa shrugged and started twirling spaghetti onto her fork.

Katie watched Mark pick at his food, pushing it around with his fork. What wasn't he telling her?

She opened her mouth to ask again if there wasn't

something he was keeping from her. But Katie felt a presence behind her even before she heard someone clearing their throat.

She turned to find Joelle Needham clutching an iPad to her oversized chest.

Katie had to bite her tongue to keep from asking Joelle if she ordered her Whitney blazer too small on purpose.

"Wow, don't you look bummed," Mark's ex-girlfriend said, her glossy lips pouting. "But I guess I'd be, too, if I knew everyone was eyeballing a pic of me naked. Good thing the lighting sucks. That hides a lot of flaws." Joelle smiled at Katie. "You should thank God for that, sweetie."

"Who's naked?" Katie looked at Mark. "What's she rambling about?"

He shook his head. "What do you want, Jo?" he asked, dropping his fork to his plate with a clatter. "Get to the point. I'm not in the mood."

Joelle frowned. "Looks like you've been caught in the act, as if you didn't know. But it's obvious Katie's still in the dark or she'd be hiding in her room at Amelia House, dying of embarrassment." She set her tablet down in front of them. "Not your best angle either, babe," she said lightly, and gave Mark's shoulder a squeeze.

Katie's gaze dropped to the screen. "OMG," she breathed. And for a second, it felt like her heart stopped.

The image was fuzzy, the lighting as bad as Joelle had mentioned. But there was no question who it was: a barenaked Mark, his eyes closed, lips parted, head back so that his neck arched, revealing the medallion caught in the hollow of his throat. As if the shadowed outlines of his features weren't enough to identify him, there was also the soaring eagle tattoo on his right bicep. Katie would have recognized it anywhere.

"Aw, don't look so sad. Cellulite's not the end of the world," Joelle said, and gave Katie a nudge. "Besides, you've got all that dark hair hanging down. You can pretend it's not you."

Katie blinked, because even she thought at first that it was her. She looked hard at the bare back and butt, the pale arms, and the brown hair falling like a thick curtain over the shoulders. The girl's head was bent as she kissed Mark's shoulder while her hand rested on his hip.

"It's not," Katie said, a sharp pain stabbing her chest. "That's not me."

Joelle put a finger to her chin. "Hmm, that was pretty good. I almost believed it. Practice saying it a few more times, and it might sound convincing."

"That's *not* me," Katie repeated, anger swelling inside her.

Tessa leaned over from the other side of the table, looking at the photo upside down. "Can't you see the tat on her hand?" she said. "Katie doesn't have any ink."

It wasn't easy to spot at first glance, but the girl in the photo had the tattoo of a red rose on her hand, its stem wrapping around her wrist.

"Oh, snap," Joelle said, squinting at her iPad and then at Katie, a tight smile playing at her lips. "You're right. It isn't you, is it?"

Though Katie was sure that Joelle had realized the truth all along.

"Well, I'll bet you two have lots to talk about," Joelle said, and reached between Katie and Mark to retrieve her tablet. "What with Mark here banging your slutty twin."

Katie stared at Mark, not even waiting for Joelle to leave before she asked, "Who *is* she?" Her voice shook, and she felt hot all over, like she had the worst fever ever.

"I think it's a girl from the party. Someone Steve brought. I barely noticed her." Mark shook his head. His face looked pinched. "I wouldn't cheat on you, Katie, I swear."

"Right, he swears," Joelle said, and tucked her iPad against her chest. She stared at Mark with what looked like hurt in her eyes. "Guess everything isn't always what it looks like, huh?"

Mark snorted. "With you, it was exactly what it looked like."

"You just wanted any excuse to bail," Joelle shot back. "You wouldn't even hear me out—"

"Let it go!" Mark stood so quickly that the bench jerked backward. "Move on, Jo, and stop with the bullshit. You know me, and this"—he poked a finger at her iPad—"isn't who I am. Someone's on a mission to make me look bad, and we both know who." Mark turned to glare at Steve Getty. "The guy's a total narcissist. It's all about him."

Joelle briefly touched Katie's shoulder. "I warned you, didn't I?"

"Mark, tell me the truth," Katie said, standing up. She'd

believed in him these past three months. Had he been with someone else?

"Good luck with that," Joelle said softly as she headed off.

"I mean it, Mark." Katie could hardly breathe. "Is it real or not?"

He flinched. "It might be real, but it's not the truth," he told her. "Steve must've set me up. It's the only thing that makes sense. He gave me a beer, the one I was drinking when I got sick and passed out—"

"Wait! What?" Katie's head spun. "You passed out?" He'd conveniently left that part out when she'd asked about the party before.

"I've been trying to piece things together, but I don't remember much before I woke up in the maid's room." There was desperation in his voice. He reached for her, clutching her fingers. "You just have to trust me."

"Trust you?" Katie had trusted him blindly until a minute ago. Now it wasn't that easy. Her hands felt like ice. She looked at Tessa, who stared back across the table, her cool blue eyes watching. "So this girl with the rose tattoo, nothing happened with her, is that what you're saying?"

"Yeah, nothing happened. At least, I don't think so." Mark's face turned red. "Like I said, I can't remember—"

"You're kidding, right?" Katie hated the high pitch of her voice. "You can't remember being in bed with a girl?"

He winced. "What I know is that Steve handed me a beer that made me sick. The last thing that sticks with me is talking to Charlie, telling him I needed air. After that"—

he shrugged—"nothing. Why would I make something like that up?"

"No clue." Katie wanted to believe him, she really did. "Is that all?" she asked, giving him one more chance.

"Yeah." The muscles in his jaw started to twitch. "That's everything I know."

The room seemed to go freakishly quiet, or was that just her mind growing still while the rest of her world fell apart in a noisy *whoosh*?

Please, she thought, *please let this be a joke. Am I getting punked?* She swallowed and looked around, only to see the curious stares and Steve Getty's smug face, gloating like a highway billboard.

"C'mon, Katie, you know I would never risk losing you. I would never do anything so stupid." Mark held her arms so tightly it hurt. "It has to be Steve. There's no other explanation. Who else would've taken that picture and made sure it was seen by everyone at Whitney?"

That made sense. It did. If only Katie could get the image of her boyfriend and that tattooed girl out of her head.

She stepped over the bench, snatching up her book bag from the floor. "I'll see you later," she said. Then she walked away, even as her legs shook beneath her.

"Katie, wait—"

But she didn't turn around.

CHAPTER EIGHT

KATIE

Katie didn't realize that she'd been holding her breath until she'd escaped the dining hall and rushed down the steps. The off-and-on drizzle had turned into a downpour. She clutched her book bag to her chest, sloshing through puddles, blinking as rain stuck her lashes together, obscuring her tears.

Students huddled under colorful umbrellas hurried past, and Katie felt invisible against their vibrant reds and yellows. Her head down, wet hair plastered to her cheeks, she fought hard to keep from sobbing.

It'll be okay, she tried to console herself, despite the knot in the pit of her stomach. She had dealt with her father's suicide without falling apart, hadn't she? That kind of loss was the worst. Death was final. That photograph of Mark and the girl with the rose tattoo might not even be real. But as hard as she tried to convince herself that Steve had set Mark up, that the whole thing was bogus, her chest ached like she'd been slammed in the ribs with a two-by-four.

Because if it *was* real, it meant that Mark had betrayed her. Lied to her. And, at the moment, she wasn't sure which was worse.

They could talk when the shock had worn off and she'd had the chance to calm down. At the moment, she was desperate to crawl into bed, bury her face in the pillow, and cry her eyes out.

The yellow facade of Amelia House loomed ahead, a bright spot in the gloom. Katie ran up the steps and inside, shutting the door loudly behind her.

The noise brought Estelle Gabbert flying out of her room. She pushed up the sleeves of her tailored shirt, penny loafers slapping the floor as she hurried into the foyer. "Please, don't slam . . . Oh!" The housemother stopped dead in her tracks when she saw a rain-drenched Katie dripping onto the doormat.

"Good heavens, Katie! You're soaked to the skin! Stay right where you are, you poor thing," she said, and disappeared into her room only to emerge seconds after with a fluffy pink towel.

Before Katie could protest, the housemother descended on her, wiping the rain off her face and rubbing her hair with the towel before draping it over Katie's shoulders.

"Thanks," Katie said, holding on to her book bag as she headed for the stairs. The last thing she wanted was to make small talk. All she wanted was to curl up and hide until she'd cried herself out.

"Hold on a minute. Something came for you this morning. I apologize for the condition it's in," Mrs. Gabbert said, "but it's about as wet as you are. It was left on the back stoop. I didn't even know it was there till I took out the trash."

"I've got a package?" Katie grabbed the banister and turned around. She hardly ever got boxes, except on rare occasions when her mom mailed her chocolate chip cookies.

"I think it was hand-delivered, though I'm not sure why it wasn't brought to the front. I looked around but didn't see anyone. Just the grounds crew across the way planting roses," the housemother was saying, when the front door banged open and Tessa appeared, slamming it behind her.

Mrs. Gabbert winced. "Can't anyone ever do anything quietly?" she muttered.

"Sorry," Tessa said, stomping wet shoes on the mat. She looked even more like a drowned rat than Katie. She pushed away the pink towel Katie offered her. "Let's go upstairs right now and talk about how you're going to totally humiliate Mark Summers when you publicly dump his ass."

"No," Katie told her, surprised how calm her voice sounded when her insides felt like Jell-O. "Mrs. G. has a package for me, and I'd like to see what it is."

"Yes, the package! I set it on the drainboard to dry." The housemom headed for the kitchen. "I'll go get it."

Katie sank down onto the bench beneath the stairwell, sliding her soggy book bag from her shoulder to the floor.

Tessa squeezed the rain out of her hair. "You look like crap," she said. "Are you sure you're okay?"

"What do you think?"

"I think you need to get over him fast." Tessa snatched the pink towel from Katie to dry off her face. "Mark might have everyone around here convinced that he's God, but he's the opposite. He's a dog, just like Steve Getty said."

"Way to kick me when I'm down," Katie murmured.

"Sometimes the truth hurts."

Katie glanced at her hands. After her dad died, she bit her nails down to the quick. When she'd gotten to Whitney, she started seeing the school shrink for weekly sessions. It had taken months of therapy and snapping rubber bands against her wrists before she'd kicked the habit. *So much for that.* She sighed and started gnawing on her thumbnail.

"I have to give him credit for one thing, at least," Tessa went on. "When you ran out, he went back to the hockey jocks' table and slammed Getty in the face. I think he might have knocked out a few teeth."

"What?" Katie stared at Tessa. "Mark hit Steve?"

"Yeah, and Steve was spitting blood. Hmm, I wonder if he had any teeth left to lose."

Katie wasn't sorry that Mark had gone after Getty. Maybe the whole thing *was* Steve's fault. Why else would Mark be convinced enough to beat him up in front of everyone in the dining hall?

Mrs. Gabbert appeared. "Here you are, hon," she chirped. "But be careful. The box is wet from the rain, and it's got a strange smell to it, like perishables that have already perished."

Katie stood up and took the box. The cardboard had been

52

soaked through so that a faded label marked TWO DOZEN BRILLO PADS could barely be read. It was held together by twine, not tape. Weird.

"Mrs. G.'s right," Tessa said, wrinkling her nose. "It smells like bologna gone bad. Who sent it?"

"I don't know." The rain had smeared the ink, making a mess of Katie's name. There was no address, not even her dorm name. There was nothing in the left-hand corner where the return address should have been, so she had no idea where it came from. "Do you think it's from Mark?"

"Would he give you rotten meat?" Tessa looked at her like she was crazy. "If he did, he's really lost it."

Katie set the package on the floor and pried off the twine. There was no note, just something rolled up in yellowed paper, something that smelled rank enough to make her hold her breath as she began to unwrap it. Toward the end, the paper unrolled all by itself and dumped the contents between her feet. *Plop.*

"Oh, my God," she whispered when she saw what it was. The few bites of lunch she'd eaten backed up in her throat.

It was a severed human hand, bone protruding from where the wrist used to be. The skin had turned a mottled shade of grayish purple, and the fingers curled like claws, with badly chipped nails once painted hot pink. On the back of the hand was a bloodred rose.

"Lord have mercy!" Mrs. Gabbert gasped.

"That can't be real, can it?" Even tough-as-nails Tessa sounded freaked out. "It's rubber, right?"

But it didn't look rubber to Katie. It didn't smell like it either. She stared at the object unraveled from the stained paper, her stomach churning. She could hardly breathe.

"Oh, God, oh, God, oh, God," she murmured over and over, turning away, unable to look a second longer.

Had someone cut off the party girl's rose-tattooed hand and delivered it to her?

"I'm calling security!" Mrs. Gabbert said in a shaky voice as she backed out of the foyer.

"I'm gonna be sick," Katie murmured, wobbling as she took a few steps away from the box. As Tessa held her arm to steady her, Katie turned her head and puked all over Tessa's shoes.

CHAPTER NINE

MARK

Mark swiped at his bloody nose with the sleeve of his blazer as he walked down the marble-tiled hallway. Just outside the closed doors to his father's office, he caught his reflection in a mirror and frowned. A purple bruise had begun forming along his jaw and drying blood clung to his nostrils. He let out a slow breath, telling himself that Steve had asked for it, that the beating was long overdue.

If Whitney Prep's head of security hadn't shown up so fast, Mark would have killed the guy. But Wharton's crew had quickly broken things up and disbanded the crowd that had gathered. One uniform had taken Getty to the school's infirmary—with Steve giving Mark a hint of a bloody smile on his way out, like he'd won the fight, not lost it—while Wharton himself had dragged Mark to the administration building. "Your father wants to see you, and he's not happy" was all he said.

Like that wasn't the understatement of the year. Mark expected Wharton to shadow him into the building, right to his father's door, but the campus security chief got a call on his walkie-talkie and sped off toward the dorms, leaving Mark to go it alone.

Mark swallowed hard as he stared at the engraved brass plate on the double doors.

HEADMASTER GREGORY M. SUMMERS, PHD.

Yep, his dad must be pretty damned pissed.

He pushed open the outer doors, entering the reception area normally manned by poodle-haired secretary Naomi. Only Naomi was nowhere in sight. Probably still out to lunch.

Almost immediately, the inner door swung wide and Greg Summers appeared, holding it open. A tall man wearing the blue uniform of the Barnard police emerged, hat in hand. "I appreciate that you came to see me first, Captain Franks," Mark's dad was saying. "I promise that campus security will look into the matter. I'll be in touch when we have any information."

"Much obliged," the police captain said, scrutinizing Mark's bruised face before he tucked his hat back on his head and left.

As soon as the outer double doors clicked shut, Mark's father hustled him into his office. He didn't say another word until he'd locked them in. Then he frowned at Mark. "Mind telling me what the hell's going on around here?"

Mark touched his aching jaw. "You want to know about the fight?"

"I want to know about *everything*."

Mark was taller than his dad and far broader in the shoulders but somehow his father still intimidated the crap out of him. "You always taught me to stand up for myself. That's all I did."

"That isn't all, Mark. You and I both know that." Gregory Summers's forehead bunched above his tortoiseshell glasses as he walked around his desk and settled into his leather chair. "Be straight with me, okay? No bullshit."

Why did it feel like this was about more than the fight? Mark sat down across from his father. "I'm here because I kicked Steve's ass, right? Has he got Ambassador Getty threatening to sue the school?"

"No one's threatening anything," his dad replied. "Steve Getty's lucky to be here, all things considered."

Mark wondered what kind of trouble Steve Getty had caused to get booted from so many boarding schools before Whitney. Was it cheating? Smoking pot? Had he stolen something? But Mark knew his dad wouldn't tell him, and whatever Steve had done wouldn't be found in his transcripts either. That was how it worked for the sons of politicians: their fathers donated a tidy sum for a new computer lab or football field and any charges of misconduct disappeared from their records.

"Steve's been an asshole since he got here," Mark said, and rubbed slick palms along the crease of his khakis. "So don't ask me to apologize—"

"Apologize?" His dad cut him off. "You think I brought you here so I could force you to tell your teammate you're sorry?" Gregory Summers sighed. "If this was just about a fight it would make things much simpler."

Mark hated seeing his dad look so upset. Not an hour ago, Katie had looked at him much the same way. How could things have changed so fast in just a few days? It had all started with the damned party. He wished like hell it had never happened.

Oh, crap. That was it, wasn't it?

"You heard about the party," Mark said, and wondered if his dad knew about the photo, too. "It wasn't any big deal. Just some guys from the hockey team celebrating."

"Really?" His dad cocked his head. "Are you sure about that?"

Mark winced. His father knew about the girls.

His nose began to drip, and he reached up with his sleeve, smearing blood on his cuff. "All right, so there may have been a couple of townies there. Steve snuck them in. I didn't know who they were. I had nothing to do with them."

"Mark," his dad said, like he didn't buy it.

"I swear," Mark said, but he was sweating.

"Then why was a Barnard police officer just in my office asking about someone named Rose Tatum who apparently went to a party at my house last Saturday night?"

"I didn't even know the girls' names," Mark said, wondering if she was the one in the photograph. "Did she steal something from the house?" He asked the first thing that came to mind. Had she stolen his medallion?

"No, that's not why Captain Franks was here." His dad took off his glasses and pinched the bridge of his nose. He looked afraid, Mark thought, really freaked out. "Rose Tatum's roommate reported her missing. She hasn't been seen since Saturday evening."

"What?" Mark shook his head, hardly able to swallow. The girl was gone? His dad couldn't possibly think he had something to do with it. "Look, I barely saw the girls," Mark said, and met his dad's eye. "Talk to Steve. He must know them. He brought them onto campus. I figured he took them home."

"I'm told you were the last to see her."

"Me?" Mark blinked, completely caught off guard. "Did Steve say that?"

"It's what the girl's roommate told the police," his father explained. "She said that when she left, Rose was 'getting busy' with the headmaster's son."

"But I didn't—" Mark started to deny the accusation, only to have his father's stare shut him up fast.

"I've seen the photo of you and the girl, courtesy of Mr. Getty. How drunk were you that night, Son?"

Mark's chest filled with red-hot anger. "I wasn't drunk! Steve handed me a beer before I passed out. He must've slipped something in my cup. There's no other explanation." Mark paused at the disappointed look on his father's face. "I'm telling the truth."

His dad's eyes narrowed on him. "You were drugged by your teammate?"

"Yes." Mark was sure of it.

"So you have proof?"

"No."

His father sighed. "I see."

But Mark could tell that he didn't. That knot in the pit of Mark's stomach kept growing. "You believe me, don't you?"

"It's not that." His dad pinched the bridge of his nose again, something he did when he was nervous and trying hard not to show it. "It's keeping everything from blowing up. You have to think harder about that night. You have to try—"

"I've tried! Steve must have spiked my beer with roofies, Special K . . . hell, I don't know, *something*," he insisted, because it was the only thing that made sense. "He's out for blood, Dad. I mean, it's never been good between us, not since his first day on campus. But I didn't know he was so hard-core. Yeah, he wants to be starting forward, not second line, so he'll get the attention of recruiters and scouts. But it's more than that. It's like he wants to take everything I have away from me."

"You can't remember anything?"

"I was talking to Charlie." Mark stood up, too frustrated to stay put. "I felt like I was about to throw up. I wanted some air. The next thing I know, it's morning, and I'm in Annalisa's room with my clothes off." He fell back into the chair, exhaling loudly. "If I'd cheated on Katie, I wouldn't forget it. I'd own up to it, you know I would. But I didn't."

"So the picture's a fake?" his dad said.

Mark shrugged. He didn't know how to answer. "I didn't participate willingly. I know that for sure."

For a long moment, his father looked at him, saying nothing. The phone started ringing, but he ignored it. When it stopped and rang again, he muttered, "Where the hell is Naomi?" But he didn't answer it. He loosened his tie and the button at his collar. "We'll figure this out," he said, but his dark eyes were grim. "It'll be okay."

"Yeah?" Mark wanted so badly to believe him.

"Maybe Rose Tatum will turn up and it'll all blow over."

Mark thought of the way the cop who'd left his dad's office had stared at him, and he swallowed hard. "The police don't think I have something to do with her disappearing?"

When his dad didn't answer, Mark shook his head.

"No way, that's crazy!"

Even as he said it—even though he believed it himself—something inside his gut twisted. Because he couldn't be one hundred percent sure, could he? The more he tried to remember, the more that night became a big, fat blank.

"Just lie low for a while," his father said. "Go to classes and to practice, then straight home. No more fights. No girls. You got it?"

"Yeah," Mark replied.

"It'll be all right, you'll see."

"Sure," Mark said without much conviction. He had a

really bad feeling about this whole thing. It wasn't like his mom leaving or his dad changing jobs; it was much, much worse and it scared him shitless.

The phone rang again. This time, his father picked it up. And Mark took the opportunity to bail.

CHAPTER TEN

TESSA

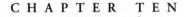

Within ten minutes of Katie opening the box and finding the hand, Amelia House was swarming with campus cops. Tessa wondered who'd show up next. The police chief from Barnard? Dr. Arnold from the cadaver lab? That tired-looking actor from *CSI: New York*?

Her chin jerked up as the French doors to the den opened, and she realized she'd left someone off her list: the school shrink.

"Dr. Capello, thanks for coming so quickly. The headmaster thought it would be a good idea for you to chat with the girls," Mrs. Gabbert said as she ushered the psychiatrist into the room where Tessa and Katie had been stashed after the security chief had finished grilling them. For some reason, he hadn't seemed at all happy with Tessa's replies.

Do you have any idea who sent the package?

Isn't it your *job to find out?*

Do you know why someone would target Miss Barton?

Because she dates that jerk Mark Summers?

Are you aware if Miss Barton has recently received any harassing emails or texts?

Does that include hurl-inducing love notes?

Tessa heard the security chief mumble "Smart-ass" under his breath.

"Can I get you anything, Lisa? Coffee, tea, water?" Mrs. Gabbert rambled on. Her face was red and she kept kneading her hands. She looked on the verge of a heart attack.

"Thanks, Estelle, but I'm good." Dr. Capello smiled thinly. "I'll take it from here if you don't mind."

"Certainly." Mrs. Gabbert nodded and left the room.

"How're you both doing?" Dr. Capello asked, and pulled a chair nearer the sofa where Tessa and Katie sat.

"I'm all right," Tessa said. "But then I'm not the one with the secret admirer." She glanced at Katie's pale face and the tissue she was pulverizing in her lap.

"How about you, Katie?" the doctor asked, sitting down and crossing her legs. Her dark hair was pulled off her face in a ponytail, and she had bangs that made her look more like a Whitney student than a grown-up. She was even wearing a burgundy jacket that was a dead ringer for their school blazers. All that was missing was the crest.

Katie turned teary eyes on the doctor. "I'm pretty freaked out. Who'd do something so twisted?"

"I don't know," Dr. Capello answered. "Someone who needs help."

"Someone who needs a padded cell, you mean," Katie said. Her fingers shook as she shredded the tissue. "What I don't get is why they'd send something like that to *me*? The security chief acted like I'd done something to bring it on."

"Don't blame yourself," Dr. Capello told her. "You can't control what other people do. It's not your fault this happened."

Katie bit her lip, nodding.

Tessa watched the exchange, keeping quiet. Every time she sat in a room with Dr. Capello she had to remind herself that no matter how caring and nice the shrink seemed, she worked for the headmaster. Everything that anyone told her wound up in a file, property of Whitney Prep.

"How do I explain this to my mom?" Katie asked, and her eyes filled with tears. "How am I ever supposed to feel safe again?"

"No place is safe," Tessa said, pushing hair behind her ears. "Anyone can find you if they really want to. All they have to do is Google. If you really don't want to be found, you have to drop off the grid like you don't exist—"

"Stop, Tessa! You're only making things worse!" Katie gave her a scathing look.

"Hey, it's not my fault! Blame Big Brother."

"It's completely normal to be afraid after what you've gone through," Dr. Capello said. "But the headmaster has campus security working overtime, and I'm sure the Barnard police will get involved as well."

"You think they'll catch whoever did it?" Katie asked.

Dr. Capello nodded. "I do."

"Get real." Tessa snorted. "People get away with stuff all the time around here. And if their parents can't buy them out of it, they just yank them from school and they start all over again somewhere else."

"You think someone from Whitney cut off that girl's hand?" Katie asked, looking horrified.

"Why's that so hard to imagine?" Tessa said, wondering how her friend could be so naive. The school was full of spoiled rich kids who'd been raised by nannies and used as pawns in their parents' divorces. To say they had issues was an understatement. "It could be anyone, right, Dr. Capello? You know things about us that no one else knows. Everyone tells you their deep, dark secrets. I'll bet some are even creepier than this."

The school shrink leveled her gaze on Tessa. "I understand why you're cynical," she said. "You've been through a lot more than most."

Maybe Dr. Capello meant to sound sympathetic, but Tessa heard only pity in her voice, and it got her back up.

"So whose hand is it?" she said, sure that Katie was wondering the same thing but was too afraid to ask. "Is it that girl in the sex pic with Mark Summers?"

"Tessa!" Katie turned a shade paler.

But Tessa didn't quit. "It's the same rose tattoo, isn't it?"

Did Katie want to pretend that there wasn't a connection? "Does anyone know her name?"

"I'm sure we'll find out soon enough," Dr. Capello replied.

Tessa turned to Katie. "Didn't your boyfriend say she was someone Steve Getty brought to his party?"

"Would you stop dogging Mark!" Katie snapped. "He had nothing to do with this."

"I didn't say he did." Tessa was a little surprised that Katie defended him, especially after what Mark had done to her.

"Drop it, okay?" Katie went to the window, pushing back the drape. There was a swirl of red and blue lights as a police car pulled up out front. "Will the cops take the box with them?"

"Yes," Dr. Capello said. "They'll need to examine it to find answers. I'm sure they'll piece everything together soon enough."

"Piece together, huh?" Katie dropped the drape. "Where's the rest of her?" she asked, a pained expression on her face. "She wasn't alive when her hand was cut off, was she?" Katie swallowed. "Whoever she is, she's dead, right?"

Dr. Capello didn't answer. "I'm just very sorry you have to deal with something as horrible as this," she said.

Tessa wanted to laugh. What a lame reply! Katie had to know the girl was dead. Otherwise, there'd be a zombie chick walking around without a hand. That was the problem with everyone at Whitney. They liked to pretend bad things didn't happen. They acted like everything was picture perfect inside the gates.

Only Tessa knew better than anyone that it wasn't true. Bad things happened to everyone, everywhere. They were just easier to hide when you had money.

"Campus security will keep an eye on Amelia House, and if you're afraid to go somewhere by yourself, an officer will tag along, okay?" Dr. Capello was saying. "If you need to talk any time, day or night, call me." She gave Katie a pat on the arm.

Katie nodded.

"You too, Tessa." The shrink turned her dark eyes on Tessa.

"Right."

Tessa just wanted everyone to go away and leave them alone.

But even after the school shrink took off and the Barnard police had removed "that nasty parcel," as she'd heard Mrs. Gabbert refer to it, the campus cops hung around Amelia House. Mrs. G. was so skittish she offered to let one of the cops sleep on the couch in the den. Tessa found that kind of funny since the Whitney rule book noted that *Boys are not allowed beyond the foyer in the girls' dormitories and may only remain there so long as the housemother is present.*

She guessed rules went out the window when a student got a box with a severed hand. Though Mrs. G. was hardly the only one flipping out.

Tessa couldn't even get Katie to leave their room for the rest of the day. The headmaster had given them permission to play hooky, and Tessa wanted to get outside once the rain stopped. "Let's hit the student center," she said. "Grab a cup of coffee and a stale doughnut. You'll feel better if we just do normal things."

"You think coffee will make me feel normal?" Katie frowned, hugging a ragged stuffed bear that she'd brought to boarding school with her. "What if the psycho's there, watching me?"

"So you're never going to leave the dorm?"

"I will when they catch him," Katie said, looking at her like she was nuts.

Katie wouldn't even go to the bathroom by herself, and she made Tessa stand guard when she took a shower that night. Even though Tessa didn't let anyone near her, Katie emerged white-faced and scared. She claimed she'd seen shadows outside the frosted glass door, like someone had walked past it, though Tessa assured her that no one had been anywhere near.

At bedtime, Katie insisted they leave the closet light on or she couldn't go to sleep. It had been such a long day and Tessa was pretty bleary-eyed, so she went along with it. She wasn't sure when they'd finally drifted off. Katie hadn't gotten off the phone with her Mom until midnight, and then she'd spent another hour texting Mark. It was still dark outside when Tessa heard Katie's whimpers.

"Tessa," her friend called, her voice quavering. "*Tessa!*"

"I'm right here," she said, flying across the room and grabbing Katie's trembling hands. "It's okay. Everything's all right."

"No." Katie shook her head, hair falling in her face. Her

eyes welled with tears. "I smelled roses again. Someone was in the room."

"No one's here but us."

"They stood by my bed, Tess!"

"Okay, okay, let me look around."

Tessa got up and made a big show of peering into the hallway and checking their closet. She even got down on all fours and peeked beneath the beds. "I swear, no one's hiding," she said, and sat down beside Katie. She brushed dark hair from Katie's face, hating the fear she saw in her friend's eyes. "Scoot over," she told her. "I'll stay here so you can get some sleep."

Katie moved nearer the wall and Tessa settled into the twin bed beside her. She turned her face so their foreheads almost touched. "You'll protect me from the psycho?"

"Like a pit bull in Joe Boxer."

Katie cracked a smile. "More like a Chihuahua."

"Ha," Tessa said. "Now go to sleep."

"Okay." Katie found Tessa's hand beneath the covers and squeezed.

Tessa didn't dare move for the longest time, not until Katie closed her eyes and her breathing became slow and deep. Tessa's heart still beat too quickly. She would never admit it, but she was shaken, too. Bad things were happening that she couldn't control, like before, with the fire.

You were just a child, the school shrink kept telling her. *You're not responsible for what happened.*

But Tessa knew differently. She *was* responsible, and she had to live with the aftermath every day of her life. Yeah, she'd been a child, but she'd done nothing to stop it. She'd known something was wrong, and she'd never spoken up. Wasn't keeping quiet sometimes a very bad thing by itself?

Katie sighed in her sleep, and Tessa whispered, "I'll be more careful this time. I can't lose anyone else."

She'd lost too much already.

CHAPTER ELEVEN

KATIE

When Katie cracked open her eyes the next morning, Tessa was already dressed and sitting at her desk, fingers tapping on her laptop.

Katie glanced at her alarm clock. It was half past eight. "Oh, God, I'm so late," she groaned, throwing off the covers.

Tessa turned her head. "Hey, you. I thought you'd never get up."

"I'm missing Nineteenth-Century American Poets," Katie said, hopping on one leg as she pulled on black tights beneath her sleep shirt. Where had she put her bra?

Tessa flashed a rare smile. "The dead poets can do without you for one morning. The headmaster gave us a pass today, too, remember?"

"Oh, crap, you're right." Katie sank onto the bed. She sighed and wiped the grit from her eyes. "I feel like I hardly slept."

"You snored like a freight train."

"I was asleep for five minutes."

"Then it just seemed like forever," Tessa teased.

Katie gave her a look that said thanks. If it hadn't been for Tessa, Katie wouldn't have slept at all. Every time she'd closed her eyes, she saw the hand, the red-rose tattoo so bright against the gray flesh.

Blech.

"What're you doing?" She pushed the ugly thought from her head and crossed the room, peering over Tessa's shoulder. "Making friends?"

"Hardly." Tessa moved her laptop screen so Katie could see the Facebook page she was looking at.

It was for a girl named Rose Tatum.

"That's her," Tessa said. "The one with the rose tat."

"Rose," Katie said, and her guts twisted. Seeing the page made the girl seem more human. She had dark hair hanging past her shoulders, almond-shaped brown eyes, and a wide mouth curved in a cryptic half smile.

"She does look like you," Tessa said.

"I don't see it."

"You just don't want to."

Okay, yeah, Katie guessed there was a vague resemblance. But it creeped her out to think she looked like a girl who was missing and probably dead. So she focused on the differences. Rose wore a lot more makeup, had crooked front teeth, and had piercings up and down her ears. Plus, there was the matter of the rose tattoo on her hand and wrist.

"It's too bad I can't friend her," Tessa said. "We could find out more about her, like which Whitney hockey jock she liked partying with most."

Katie ignored Tessa, reading Rose's public info: she was single, worked as a waitress at the Barnard Diner, and had 267 friends. Her favorite quote was attributed to Snooki: "I'm not trashy unless I drink too much."

"Typical." Tessa sniffed. "Girls like her ask for trouble. Doesn't it seem like they always end up OD'ing or something?"

Katie flashed back on the hand in the box and shivered. "Nobody asks for that, Tessa. No one."

But Tessa wasn't done. "Why would a nineteen-year-old waitress want to party with prep school jocks?"

"Um, because they're rich and cute," Katie said, stating the obvious.

"They're spoiled and conceited," Tessa countered. "Girls like Rose are Kleenex to guys like Steve Getty. They use them, then toss them."

"Even if that's true, she and Steve still could have had a thing. Maybe she helped him set up Mark. Except we might never find out," Katie said, and reached over Tessa's shoulder to close Rose's Facebook page. "I can't look anymore."

"Well, you'd better get used to seeing her picture. The police posted a missing-persons flyer downstairs and they've got it up on the school's website, too. They're nosing around again this morning, asking if anyone's run into her since last Saturday."

The Barnard police had shown up yesterday before Dr.

Capello left, wanting to fingerprint Katie and Tessa and Mrs. Gabbert. "So we can rule you out when we examine the box," the cop had explained. But it had made Katie feel like a criminal, having her fingers rolled in ink and pressed onto an index card. She could still see the purple residue on her skin.

"Everyone's talking, you know." Tessa hesitated, though she looked fit to burst. "Word is that Mark was the last one to see Rose alive."

"Stop," Katie said sharply, and wrapped her arms around her stomach. Maybe the school gossips were getting off on this whole mess but Mark was scared out of his mind. He'd sent her text after text last night, telling her about the police showing up at his dad's office and how he was under suspicion.

> i didn't do anything! i didn't hurt that girl.
> you have to believe me!

Katie could only text back:

> I want to.

At the moment, she wasn't sure of anything. Her world had turned upside down again, just like when her dad died. But Katie wasn't about to shut down this time. She didn't feel depressed. She wasn't even scared anymore. She was angry. Right when she'd found a guy she really loved—when she'd opened up her heart—someone seemed to be trying their best to take it all away.

Within hours after Katie had opened The Box, the

headmaster had shot an email to the student body and their parents about a "disturbing item" having been sent to a student and requesting that anyone with any information contact campus security. He'd instituted a nine p.m. curfew as well. Katie's mom had called her right after hearing directly from the headmaster about the incident.

"Are you okay?" she'd asked, clearly upset. "Should I come and get you? Do you want to come home?"

Katie was tempted to pack her bags and leave this whole mess behind—to forget about the hand and Rose Tatum and Mark and that disgusting photo she couldn't get out of her head. But Katie knew she couldn't go. As confused as she was about Mark, she wouldn't bail on him, not when the Barnard police considered him the prime suspect in Rose Tatum's disappearance. If she really loved him, she owed it to him to stick around until Rose was found. And she would.

"I want to stay," she'd told her mom. "I'll be careful, I promise."

"Oh, baby, this makes me so uneasy! Text me every day, all right? And if you change your mind, I'll fly up there."

"Okay," Katie had told her, but she hoped it wouldn't come to that. Graduation was only six weeks away. It would suck to take off before then. *The police are doing everything they can to find whoever's responsible,* the headmaster had told her. *The campus police are cooperating fully. You'll be as safe here as anywhere.*

Katie hoped he was right.

"Where is she?" Tessa asked, drawing Katie back to the present. "You think they'll find her on campus?"

"I don't know," Katie said, but she wondered, too. If Rose was dead, where was her body? What had gone on the night of the party? Who had hurt her, and why had they cut off her hand and left it for Katie at Amelia House? Was it some kind of threat?

Someone knocked on the door, and Katie nearly jumped out of her skin.

"Katie?" Mrs. Gabbert poked her gray head in. "There's a police detective downstairs to see you. If you want me to tell him to come back—"

"No, I'll come down," Katie said. She'd been expecting it. They'd interviewed Tessa the day before after fingerprinting her, but Katie hadn't been up to it.

She finished dressing and pulled her hair into a ponytail.

"I'll go with you." Tessa started to get up, but Katie shook her head.

"I should do this alone."

The detective was waiting for her in the den, underneath a portrait of Amelia Whitney, who frowned down at him. He stood as Katie entered. "I'm sorry to bother you," he said. "I know you're upset, but I have a few questions to ask you if it's okay."

"It's okay." She wasn't going to puke on anyone's shoes today.

Katie took a seat, and he passed over a photograph. It was the profile picture from Rose Tatum's Facebook page.

"Did you ever see her around campus?" he asked. "Maybe with another student?"

"No, never," Katie told him. It was the truth.

"But you *have* seen her before, haven't you?"

Katie squirmed. "Not in person."

He cocked his head. "But you did see a photograph?"

Oh, God. Katie's hands went cold. Of course he knew about the sex pic. Everyone on campus did. "Yes," she admitted. She could hardly meet his eyes.

"You know about the party she attended at the headmaster's house last Saturday night?"

"Yes," Katie said, though the word seemed to stick in her throat.

"You're dating Mark Summers."

The way he said it wasn't a question.

Katie almost said "I *was*" but caught herself.

"Yes." They'd been together three months. She'd planned to follow him to whichever university he picked from the half a dozen dangling scholarships. If she had to, she'd attend community college just to be near him. But what would happen now? Would all those plans fall apart?

"What did he tell you about Rose?" the detective asked, watching her so intently that Katie was afraid to twitch. "About what happened last Saturday night?"

"Nothing." Katie's mouth was so dry. "He barely knew her. He didn't even meet her until the party. You should be talking to Steve Getty. He's the one who snuck her onto campus. He's the reason Mark blacked out and can't remember."

"Uh-huh."

Didn't the police believe that Mark was drugged? Had

they talked to Steve or Charlie? Had they interviewed the other hockey players at the party? Katie needed to know more about what was going on.

"Tell me that at least she was dead before her hand was cut off," Katie said.

The detective nodded. "It was definitely postmortem."

"Did you find any fingerprints on the box?" she asked. "Anything to help you solve this fast?" On *CSI*, they were always pulling up matches in a blink.

"All I can safely tell you is we've taken your prints out of the equation, as well as Miss Lupinski's and Mrs. Gabbert's." He shifted in his seat. "As for other prints on the box and the wrapping, it's very much an ongoing investigation. Things take time," he insisted.

"So that's it?" Katie said. "Are we done?"

"For now."

"I hope you find her," Katie told him, and stood. "And I hope you catch the twisted person who sent me her hand."

"I intend to," he said, and tucked the photo back into a manila folder.

Katie started to walk away.

"Do one thing for me?" the detective asked, and she stopped. "Keep your eyes and ears open. If you see or hear anything that might help us, call straightaway."

"I will." Katie was determined to find answers, one way or another. She reached for the handle on the French door.

"Oh, and Miss Barton—"

"Yes?" She turned around.

"One of our guys will patrol campus until this thing's over. So if anything odd comes up, someone will always be close."

"Thanks," she said, and meant it.

Katie definitely kept her eyes open, wide enough to see the Barnard cop car roll past Amelia House several times that day and every day after throughout the next week. She was on the alert for "odd" things, too, like the comments on her Facebook page by a few of the school's better-known jerks, saying things like, u need a hand with ur lit essay? And hey k8e i'll bet ur bf is a real handyman!

Much as Katie wanted to pretend things were normal, her nerves were on edge.

She slept like crap and woke up in the dark every night, seeing shadows and smelling roses. She went to class, studied in the library (though she avoided the upper stacks), and let Tessa drag her to the student center for bad coffee and stale doughnuts. She texted her mom every day to say I'm OK, and she watched people in a way she hadn't before.

She noticed that Charlie Frazer was suddenly going out of his way to avoid her. Whenever she saw him and waved, he'd cross the grass or duck into a building so he wouldn't have to pass her. Every time she turned around in AP Biology, she caught Steve Getty watching her with a barely there smile on his face, like he knew something she didn't know. One day, Katie lingered at her desk after class, waiting for Steve to leave first. Then she'd followed him as he'd crossed campus and snuck up on Joelle Needham while she sat on a bench near the library. He'd slipped his arms around her, and

Joelle had jumped, spilling books from her lap. She looked fit to cry and pushed Steve away. Whatever she said to him made his face screw up, and he'd stomped away, hands in pockets, looking truly pissed.

Tessa seemed to be even more out of sorts than usual, too. Several times when Katie's weird dreams had awakened her in the middle of the night Tessa wasn't in her bed. When Katie asked where she went, Tessa got defensive. "I watch TV down in the media room. Is that all right with you, or do I need a permission slip?"

Weird, maybe. But nothing worth reporting to the police.

Katie hardly saw Mark the entire week after The Box, but he texted her all the time. Under orders to lie low, he told her. I miss u.

She missed him, too. They hadn't broken up, but they weren't together, not the way they had been. And all because of this mess with Rose.

No one's seen her in a week, Mark texted. Where is she?

I don't know, Katie replied. But someone must.

Yeah, but WHO???

Katie wondered the same thing. Because someone *had* to know what had happened to Rose. But whoever it was obviously wasn't talking.

The only talk Katie did hear was gossip. She couldn't even go to the toilet without getting an earful. One night when she was just about to flush, she caught two girls dissing Mark.

"If it happened by accident, you know, like rough sex, why wouldn't he just dump her somewhere no one could find her?" one of them said. "Why would he chop off her hand and give it to his girlfriend?"

"He plays hockey," the other remarked. "Those guys are vicious."

Katie was about to flush the toilet and throw open the door to confront them when she heard the *tip-tap* of heels across the tile floor and then Joelle Needham's angry voice.

"Mark Summers might be a smug bastard, but he doesn't rough up girls. *Ever.* So maybe you should just shut up."

"Sorry, Joelle," the girls murmured.

"Yeah, you are."

When it was quiet again, Katie flushed and stepped out of the stall, thinking she was alone in the bathroom.

Only Joelle was still there, staring into the mirror, tears bright on her cheeks.

Katie was about to ask if she was okay when Joelle sniffled and wiped the damp from her face. "So you heard that?" she said.

"Yeah."

"Stupid frosh. They don't know which side of their butts to wipe." Joelle leaned toward the mirror, using her pinky to clean up smeared mascara.

"Thanks for sticking up for Mark." Katie went to the sink and washed her hands. "You didn't have to do that."

Joelle tugged her auburn hair over her shoulder. "Mark might not be mine at the moment, but I know who he is. He may be vicious on the ice, but he wouldn't hurt that girl, not even if he was ripped out of his mind. He's not the one who likes it rough." She stopped and held on to the rim of the sink. "Tell Mark something for me, okay? He won't listen to anything I say."

"Sure."

Joelle pursed her lips for a moment. "Tell him I didn't want it to happen. That it wasn't what he thought."

Katie shook her head. "I don't understand."

"Mark will." Joelle's hands were shaking. "Look, it's late. Go to bed, Katie. You've got bags under your eyes. You need sleep."

Joelle walked out with a *clip-clop* of heels. The bathroom door slapped closed, leaving Katie standing there wondering what the heck had just happened.

He's not the one who likes it rough.

Who was Joelle talking about? There were at least forty guys in their graduating class alone. But the first name that came to mind was *Steve Getty.*

CHAPTER TWELVE

KATIE

Katie hurried back to her room fit to bursting, expecting to find Tessa at her desk. Her friend's laptop sat open, but Tessa was nowhere in sight. Katie tried not to worry. Tessa had always been restless, and it had gotten worse since The Box.

She leaned across Tessa's desk to glance out the window. It wasn't long before she spotted the police cruiser. As she watched it ease past the dorm, Katie jostled Tessa's MacBook and woke the screen. "Three Dead in Local House Fire" read the headline. It was an article from the *Barnard Gazette* dated ten years back.

Katie glanced toward the door, then opened the window full screen.

Emergency responders were called to a burning house on Mayfield Avenue in Barnard at 1:45 a.m. A spokeswoman for the Barnard Township Fire Department said two engines attended the scene, adding that "the fire was well developed on arrival."

According to Barnard Fire Chief Wilson Bradford, the house was centuries old with a wood shingle roof, which fed the flames. When the fire was finally extinguished, the remains of two adults and one child were recovered from the rubble. A little girl was found crying in the backyard but appeared unhurt. A neighbor, John Shillings, spotted her wandering around in her pajamas, barefoot. "It was chaos by the time the fire trucks arrived," Mr. Shillings said. "There was so much smoke you could hardly see the end of your nose. How that child made it out safely, I don't know. She must have a guardian angel."

The fire chief noted that the house suffered "irreparable damage" and would almost certainly require condemnation, as the structure was unsafe. An investigation will be conducted into the origin of the blaze.

The homeowners, John and Tanya Lupinski, had two adopted children, Peter, 12, and Tessa, 7. Mr. Lupinski, 62, had recently retired as head groundskeeper for Whitney Preparatory Academy. His wife, 50, had worked in food services at the private boarding school. According to neighbors, their children were adopted from an orphanage in Russia five years prior.

Tessa Lupinski appears to be the only survivor of the fire.

Funeral service arrangements are said to be pending.

Katie scrolled down to find a brief mention in the *Gazette* dated a week later:

The fire that destroyed the Mayfield Avenue home of John and Tanya Lupinski is being investigated as a possible arson. An accelerant was apparently used to intensify the flames, possibly to cover up a home invasion. The bodies of Mr. and Mrs. Lupinski and their 12-year-old son, Peter, were recovered, but the exact cause of death will be difficult if not impossible to determine due to the extremely poor condition of the remains, according to Barnard County medical examiner Dr. Albert Arnold.

"At this point, we're unable to tell if anything was stolen from the house prior to the fire. Evidence gathering is difficult at best considering what we have to work with," said Chief Walter Henderson of the Barnard PD. "We have asked neighbors to report any suspicious activity, and we urge anyone in the area who thinks they may have seen something to call the department and report it."

Virginia Cottingham, a longtime neighbor, said, "I wouldn't be surprised if the boy started the fire. He was always causing grief for those poor people, stealing things, running away, bringing home all sorts of riffraff. They did everything they could for him and his sister but those kids were damaged goods from day one. It's a tragedy it had to end this way."

The surviving member of the family, Tessa Lupinski, 7, has been placed in the care of the state as authorities try to locate any relatives. Dr. Gregory Summers, headmaster of Whitney Preparatory Academy, where both Mr. and Mrs. Lupinski were employed for many years, recently instituted a scholarship in their names. The first such scholarship will be given to Tessa Lupinski when she reaches 11, the minimum age for girls to attend the Whitney school.

So Dr. Arnold had been the medical examiner at the time of the fire. Katie realized now that was how he'd known to call Tessa "Miss Lupinski" when she'd stepped up to the corpse at the cadaver lab. No wonder he'd looked surprised that she had volunteered.

There were photographs alongside both articles, one of the charred remains of a house and another of the Lupinski family. That one looked like a picture from a Christmas card with everyone in turtlenecks and Mom and Dad smiling uncomfortably. Tessa looked like a smaller version of herself. She and Peter had the same fair hair and skin, the same stoic expression.

Katie's mind raced. Why was Tessa reading old articles about the fire? Was she thinking about it more lately because of The Box and the missing girl?

"Snoop much?"

Katie's cheeks warmed. She slowly turned to see Tessa standing in the doorway holding a half-eaten apple. "I wasn't snooping," she said. "I bumped your Mac and the stuff about the fire came up. I was curious."

"You know what can happen to curious cats. It usually doesn't end well." Tessa tossed the apple in the trash bin and brushed past her. "So are you done prying?" She shut down the laptop and gave Katie an icy-blue stare. "Or do you want to read my diary next?"

"I'll pass."

Tessa plopped down on her bed, tucking her legs up to her chest and hugging them. She looked like she was making herself as small as possible.

"C'mon, Tessa, don't be like that. You're my best friend. I'm worried about you," Katie said. "If you've started thinking about the fire again—"

"I'm always thinking about the fire!" Tessa snapped, and her cheeks flushed. "I have to live with what happened every day of my life. It never goes away."

"It must suck keeping it all in," Katie said, and reached for Tessa, but Tessa jerked away. "Why won't you let me help?"

"How?"

"Really talk about it for once." Katie gingerly sat on the edge of the bed. It broke her heart to see tough-as-nails Tessa looking like a scared little girl. "Get it out. You keep everything so bottled up. Someday you're going to pop."

"What do you want me to say?" Tessa asked. "That it was terrifying, watching the house burn? That I would have turned to ashes, too, if no one had heard me screaming?"

"But you did survive! You had a guardian angel that night," Katie said, repeating the words from the article. "Did you ever find out who it was?"

Tessa tucked her chin against her knees, so Katie could barely hear her. "I think it was a ghost," she whispered. "Sometimes I wish he'd left me there. . . ."

"No!" Katie reached out again. This time, Tessa didn't recoil. "Don't ever say that. If you'd died that night, who would have shown me the ropes when I was a newbie? Who else would have put up with me bawling night after night when I first arrived? I was so messed up, but you kept me going." Katie slid her fingers through Tessa's and squeezed. "You saved *my* life."

"You *were* a disaster." Tessa sniffed. "Someone had to look out for you."

"Well, I'm glad it was you." Katie looked into Tessa's face and saw her tough-girl mask soften. "Tell me something about your mom and dad, just something small that you remember. My dad loved doing stupid jigsaw puzzles. He'd have a new one every weekend for us to put together. It used to drive me crazy." Katie let out a breath. "Now I miss it."

Tessa didn't raise her eyes. At first, Katie wasn't sure she was going to answer.

"It was a long time ago, and I was little," Tessa said, very softly. "But I remember our mom smelled like flowers, and it wasn't perfume. She had a garden. She let Peter and me help her sometimes. We planted seedlings and cut flowers to put on the table. It was the only time when we were together that I thought she was happy." A light flickered in Tessa's eyes before it went out again. "Our dad was tough. He worked a lot, so he wasn't around much. He'd bring Peter with him to campus on the weekends. I always wanted to go." She bit her bottom lip. "But Peter said it wasn't fun, that he made him do all sorts of work. He used to run off when our dad wasn't looking. He found a lot of places to hide."

"What was Peter like?" Katie asked, feeling good that Tessa was opening up. In the four years they'd roomed together, she'd never gotten Tessa to say much of anything about her family.

Tessa closed her eyes, and Katie wondered if she'd pushed too much.

"I'm sorry, I don't want to make you sad," she said, holding on tighter to Tessa's hand. "Are you okay? Are *we* okay?"

Tessa opened her eyes and raised her chin from her knees. "Yeah, Dr. Phil, we're okay." She let go of Katie's hand. "But I'm beat. So if you don't mind . . ."

"Sure."

Katie got up, and Tessa crawled into bed without changing out of her clothes. She turned toward the wall and sighed. Clearly, she didn't want to talk anymore.

Katie undressed quietly and pulled on a soft tee and old sweats. Then she climbed into bed with her phone. Before she shut it off for the night, she texted her mom to say I'm OK. Luv u. Then she read a few texts from friends like Bea Lively, asking if she was doing all right. And there were four new messages from Mark.

i miss u

i need u

i love u

can i c u 2 nite?

Katie stared at the screen. She wanted so badly to be with Mark again, but she wasn't sure the time was right. Even his dad wanted them to keep their distance until Rose Tatum reappeared and this mess was cleared up, along with Mark's reputation.

She switched off her phone and pressed her cheek into her pillow. Drawing in a deep breath, she closed her eyes, hoping sleep would come fast. Only when it did, it brought the same vivid nightmare. The floor sighed, gently creaking as footsteps crossed the room. A shadow hovered over her bed, and she breathed in the smell of roses and something dank and musty.

Kay-tee. She heard her name in that weird, strangled whisper. Then she heard another whisper. *Get out,* it said. *This has to stop.*

Wake up, wake up, wake up, Katie told herself, fighting to surface.

She opened her eyes in time to glimpse pale skin and pale hair through the dark.

"Tessa?" she said groggily, hearing hushed footsteps and then the click of the door being opened and shut. *"Tessa?"*

Katie switched on the light but saw no one, just Tessa's empty bed and a dark red spot on the floor. *Is it blood?* she thought, and went closer. No, not blood, she realized, but a bloodred rose petal. She picked it up and rubbed it between her fingers, her pulse thumping. It was real.

Was her dream not a dream at all? Had someone been standing by her bed? Was it Tessa? What was going on?

Katie shoved on shoes, grabbed her phone, and ran into the empty hallway.

The door to the rear steps sat ajar, a strip of light shining through. Katie pushed it wide and entered the back stairwell. The soft tap of footsteps drifted up from below. Tessa was going down to the basement.

Without thinking, Katie followed, descending to the

bottom of the stairwell. She found herself standing in the laundry room in total darkness. She stood still a moment, letting her eyes grow accustomed to the pitch-black. Then she caught the faint beam of a penlight at the door to the machine room, past the laundry.

"Tessa?" she said, her voice rising. But no one answered.

And the beam of light disappeared.

Tessa hadn't come down to watch TV, had she? Katie had a sinking feeling she knew where her roommate was going.

Nerves tingling, she turned on her phone and used it as a flashlight. Ignoring the Do Not Enter sign, she pushed open the door to the machine room and eased her way around the furnace and hot-water tanks.

She didn't see Tessa, but she did find the metal grate shoved aside. It was in pretty much the same place as the one Mark had taken her through in the headmaster's basement. She knew it led into the underground tunnels. Tessa's dad had been head groundskeeper at Whitney when she was a kid. Had she learned about the tunnels then? Did she use them to escape when things got bad, the same way Mark did?

Maybe it was stupid—maybe Katie should let Tessa go and head back to bed—but she couldn't, not after seeing those articles about the fire and seeing Tessa's face when she'd mentioned her brother. Katie was worried about her.

So she held out the light from her phone, took a deep breath, and stepped through the opening.

Like Alice in Wonderland, down the rabbit hole she went.

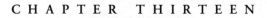

CHAPTER THIRTEEN

KATIE

Katie followed what looked like a firefly bouncing yards ahead as she fumbled her way through the steam tunnels. She touched damp walls and stumbled over loose mortar and stone, trying hard to keep her footing and not fall too far behind.

"Tessa!" she called out, but the light just kept moving.

Why was Tessa roaming underground in the dead of night? And why didn't she wait when Katie hollered? Why had she run? Was she all right?

Katie breathed in the dank smell of the earth and wished she were anywhere else. She had no idea where she was beneath the campus. When she'd been in the tunnels before, she'd had Mark to guide her. She just hoped that if she didn't catch Tessa, she could find her way back to the basement of Amelia House alone.

It wasn't long before she realized she wasn't following anyone. She'd lost the flickering penlight completely. The only thing she had to show her the way was the glow of her phone, and it was hardly very bright.

Katie stood still, hearing nothing but her ragged breaths, a soft scurrying—rats?—and the *drip drip* of water down the crumbling stone. *It's okay,* she told herself. *You didn't go far. Just backtrack and you'll be fine.* Only she hadn't been paying attention to anything but the darting light. So she didn't know which way to go when the tunnel abruptly forked.

Had she come from the left or the right?

Oh, crap.

She swallowed hard. Her heartbeat raced.

What had possessed her, following Tessa down here? No one knew where she was. If she got lost, who would even think to look for her in the tunnels?

In a panic, she hit speed dial for Mark, but the call failed. She tried Tessa's phone and then Bea Lively's with the same result. And then the screen went from dim to dark. Damn. She hadn't remembered to charge her battery in days.

A drop of water plopped onto her face, and she wiped it away.

She just had to keep walking, right? She'd find a way out sooner or later, wouldn't she? Or else she'd end up like the lost boy she'd heard about her freshman year. A student had gotten hopelessly lost in the tunnels years and years ago, or so the story went, and his ghost still wandered the maze beneath the school. If you listened hard, some said, you could hear his moans through the vents.

Katie found it hard to breathe. She felt claustrophobic and trapped. *Come on, keep going,* she told herself, moving faster, but the loose rock beneath her shoes made her slip. With a cry, she went down on hands and knees. The rough ground bit into her palms. Her knees felt scraped through her old sweatpants.

Her skin stung and her eyes blurred with tears, but she got up, reaching out for the wall to steady herself. Stone and loose mortar crumbled beneath her touch as she stood.

Though she was breathing hard, she heard loud breaths that weren't her own. She inhaled a smell that wasn't musty tunnel. More like sweat and testosterone.

Katie.

Oh, God, was it the voice from her dream? Maybe she was still asleep. *Please, please, let it be that. Let me still be in bed.*

Katie squished her eyes closed, murmuring, "Wake up, wake up, wake up," over and over. Then she heard the soft crunch of approaching footsteps.

Her eyes flew open.

Someone else was there, and she wasn't dreaming. She was lost in the tunnels and she wasn't alone.

Katie froze as something touched her hair. It was like the ghost in the library all over again. She opened her mouth to scream, but before she could make a sound, a hand clamped over her mouth, smothering the sound.

"Katie, it's me."

Mark?

Katie recognized his voice and stopped struggling. She heard a tiny click, and a penlight came on. He shined it on his face so she could see him. Then he lifted his hand from her mouth. Though her heart still hammered, suddenly she wasn't afraid. She was pissed. "What're you doing here?" She smacked his arm with her phone. "You scared me half to death!"

"I should ask you the same thing," he said, not answering her question. "Why the hell are you in the tunnels? I thought you hated them."

"I *do*," she insisted, rubbing arms covered in gooseflesh. She couldn't imagine roaming the tunnels alone, like Mark. It was beyond creepy. "I was worried about Tessa, so I followed her down——" She stopped herself, suddenly unsure of how much to say.

"Tessa's in the tunnels?" Mark frowned.

"Somewhere, I guess." Katie sighed with frustration. "She's been thinking about the fire. She was pretty upset before she went to bed. Maybe you could help me find her. . . ."

Mark made a noise. "If Tessa knows the tunnels, we could hunt for weeks and never find her, not unless she wanted us to."

"What if she's in danger?" Katie said, wondering why Mark wasn't more concerned. A girl had disappeared from a party at the headmaster's house. What if Tessa got snatched, too?

"Tessa can take care of herself," he said quietly. "You're the one who needs to be more careful. You shouldn't have come by yourself."

"But I was worried about her!" Katie didn't need a lecture. She just wanted to get out of there. She was starting to shiver.

"Well, I'm worried about *you*," Mark said, and took her hand. "Let's get you somewhere warm. I'll take you home after, I promise. I'm headed to the greenhouse. It's not far."

He wanted her to go with him to the greenhouse? The only place Katie wanted to go was back to her dorm. "Mark, I don't think—"

"Please," he said, "unless you're afraid."

Katie wasn't sure if he was asking if she was afraid of the tunnels or of him. At that moment, she was way more scared of being stranded underground than being alone with him.

"Don't lose me, okay?" she said, giving him her answer. She didn't want to get stuck in the tunnels. She couldn't imagine having to stay down there much longer. It felt like being buried alive.

"I won't lose you, I promise."

She caught a glimpse of a smile as he moved around her. Katie grabbed the back of his sweatshirt and held on as he navigated the passageway. Soon they were at the greenhouse grate.

Mark offered her a leg up, and Katie reached for the edges of the hole.

Then she pulled herself up and over, sprawling onto the greenhouse floor.

She sighed with relief at the sight of the moonlight spilling in through the glass panels. The warm, damp air settled on her skin like dew, and sweat trickled down her back beneath her T-shirt.

Mark emerged far more gracefully. He tucked his flashlight

into the pocket of his hoodie as they walked through rows of plants. When he headed toward the far corner where the rosebushes bloomed, Katie didn't follow.

He turned around. "What's wrong?"

A prickle of fear raced up Katie's spine. She told herself it had nothing to do with being alone with Mark. It was something else. She thought of the rose petal she'd found on the floor by her bed and all the times before when she'd smelled roses in her sleep. Did Tessa have something to do with that? Was Tessa *trying* to scare her? It didn't make sense.

"Sometimes I get the feeling someone's watching me," she said, because that was the only way she could explain it.

"I feel that way, too, in the tunnels sometimes." Mark glanced around, walking toward her. "But no one else is here now."

"How do you know?" She looked down the length of the greenhouse, at the rows of plants that seemed to go on forever; at the glass walls and ceiling that would be so easy to peer through. There was a muted *shhh* every time the mister went on, rustling leaves.

"I just know," he said, nodding toward a slim wooden bench. "C'mon, sit."

Katie wasn't so sure. But she rubbed the goose bumps on her arms and settled down beside him.

"I've missed you," Mark said softly. She saw the play of emotions on his face, made more dramatic by the shadows. "It's been a rough week."

"How're you holding up?" she asked.

He gave her a sad half smile. "That's what I should be asking you." He shook his head. "I'm sorry, Katie. I'm sorry for everything."

Instinctively, she touched his hand. "You didn't cause this."

"I feel like I did." Mark stared off into the distance. He looked so serious. "Maybe it's karma kicking me in the ass because I had it too good and I took it all for granted."

"No," Katie said, remembering what Dr. Capello had told her. "You didn't bring this on any more than I did. Someone out there is seriously sick."

"And not in a good way."

"I know you didn't send me the hand," she told him, something she'd believed from the start. Mark was a lot of things, but he wasn't bat-shit crazy.

"No."

"You didn't cheat on me either, did you?" she said, wondering if he would hesitate before he answered. But he didn't even pause.

"No." His voice was ragged. His eyes glistened as he turned to her. He looked so frustrated and so *vulnerable,* which wasn't a word Katie had ever associated with him. "It's like one night wrecked my whole life, and I don't know how to fix it."

"Hey," she said, and touched his cheek. "Don't give up."

"I keep trying to remember what happened at the party. I feel like I know something more, but I'm not sure how to get it out."

"Give it time," Katie whispered.

"But I don't have time! The police interviewed me for two hours the other day, Katie. Two freaking hours! They took my prints and swabbed my cheek for a DNA test. I hope they tested Steve, too."

"You honestly believe he hurt Rose? That he cut off her hand?" Katie shivered. Yeah, Steve Getty was a total douche. But lots of guys were, and it didn't mean they could murder someone.

"It wasn't me," Mark said, "it couldn't have been."

"They'll find whoever did it," Katie told him, though it sounded lame even to her ears. "At least you have a lot of support."

"Really?" Mark let out a bitter laugh. "Doesn't seem like it."

"You've got Charlie," Katie said, because he was Mark's closest friend. Maybe Charlie was avoiding her, but he couldn't possibly be avoiding Mark, too.

Mark rubbed his hands together. "Charlie's been acting strange."

"I heard Joelle defend you."

"No way." He laughed. "Was she high?"

"She was really upset," Katie said, recalling the tears on Joelle's cheeks. "She said you won't listen to her but what you saw wasn't how things happened."

"Oh, man. She's even working you now, trying to convince me she didn't cheat." He rubbed his hands over his face, shaking his head. "She's wrong. I know what I saw. She had her skirt up and Getty was on top of her, going at it. He sent her roses the next day, or so I heard."

Roses.

Katie shivered. "That doesn't mean she wanted it, you know."

Mark sighed. "Joelle doesn't take crap from anyone. She's tough."

"But she's a size two," Katie reminded him. "Steve's big, like you. Maybe he drugged her, too."

"You don't really think— Aw, damn," Mark started, then stopped and exhaled. "If he raped her, why didn't she report it? Why would she keep her mouth shut?"

Katie could think of a million reasons. "Maybe she was scared. Maybe she didn't think anyone would believe her. You didn't."

Mark pinched his eyes closed. "My father said something after I fought with Steve in the dining hall. Like, Steve's dad wouldn't argue because Steve was lucky to be at Whitney."

"What if he's done it before?" Katie said, heart thumping. "What if he did it again?"

"To Rose, you mean?" Mark let out a slow breath. "If I hadn't passed out, if I could've stayed awake, maybe things would be different. Maybe Rose would be okay, and I wouldn't be so alone in this."

"Hey." Katie nudged him. "You've got me."

"Do I?" he whispered.

He sounded so sad, it broke her heart.

I'm sorry. It'll be okay. Don't give up, she wanted to say. But the words seemed too cliché.

Katie didn't know how to comfort him. She didn't understand what was going on any more than he did. She wanted to trust him completely again, to go back to the way they were. God, but she was tired. She put her head on his shoulder, leaning into him as his arm came around her.

They didn't say much more, just sat like that until light crept across the inky sky and Katie realized they had to get moving.

As she stood, she heard faint noises—voices and an occasional dog's bark—from beyond the greenhouse, somewhere across the creek.

"What is it?" Mark asked.

"No clue." She went up to the tempered-glass wall that dripped with condensation and rubbed a circle to see through. She peered ahead to where the woods began. The glow of flashlights bumped along as dark figures meandered through the trees. She wondered what they were doing. It was way too early for a leisurely stroll.

Mark came up behind her, his breath soft in her hair.

"Oh, man, it's the search dogs. They're looking for the body," he said, and Katie felt her skin turn to goose bumps again. "They're looking for Rose."

CHAPTER FOURTEEN

MARK

Mark barely made it to hockey practice that morning before his first class. He'd slept badly after leaving Katie at Amelia House and returning through the grate in his basement. Though he'd gone back to bed, he kept thinking he heard the search dogs barking and wondered if they'd found Rose's body.

When he saw his father at breakfast, he asked if they'd turned up anything. His dad shook his head. "Nothing yet," he said grimly.

When Mark finally got to the rink, there wasn't the usual trash talk in the locker room. In the days before a big game, the team could get pretty rowdy, banging pads, pounding lockers, making noise about kicking ass. "Eye of the tiger!" someone was always yelling. There was no game bigger for Whitney than the prep school state championship. But the locker room had turned into a library with everyone speaking in hushed voices, or at least they whispered whenever Mark came around. He felt less part of the team than odd man out.

They looked at him with narrowed eyes, as though he'd done something wrong when all he'd tried to do was throw a party for his friends.

"Summers," someone called out as Mark reached into his locker for his helmet. "Yo, Mark, you deaf or what?"

"Sorry, bro, just thinking," he said as Charlie waddled over in his goalie's gear. He had his helmet cocked back on his head so the cage covered his forehead but not his face. He wore a white practice jersey, while Mark wore black. Usually, they played together, but this morning they were on opposite sides in the scrimmage.

"You ready?" his friend asked, leaning on his stick.

"Almost," Mark said, nodding down at his feet. "Just lacing up the skates."

"You doing all right?" Charlie asked, and shifted on his feet. "It's got to be hard, everyone talking about you and Rose."

"It sucks." Mark sighed, glancing up. "It's like I've got dog crap on my shoes and no one wants to smell it." *Including you,* he wanted to add, but didn't.

Charlie frowned. "That's harsh."

"Getty loves it, I'm sure."

"Speaking of dog shit," Charlie murmured. "You keeping a safe distance from him, outside the rink, I mean?"

"As much as I can." Mark had done his best to avoid Steve

Getty since the fight. It sucked that he had to deal with the guy at practice.

"I heard the cops are back on campus," Charlie said, rubbing the bump on his nose. "Did they get a tip or something?"

"They've got dogs sniffing for the body," Mark told him.

"The body," Charlie repeated, and released a slow breath. "So she's really dead?"

"Hard to imagine her walking around without a hand, bro," Mark said. "I just hope they find her soon and prove I had nothing to do with it."

"You didn't do it, man. You didn't mess her up," Charlie said, and there was something in his voice that made Mark stop lacing his skates and look up.

"Did you see something that night, Charlie? Did Steve hurt that girl? Did *I* do something?"

"Whoa, what?" His friend's eyes went wide. He shook his head. "I didn't see squat, man."

Voices suddenly rose in the next aisle as lockers slammed, and Mark saw Steve and a couple of other guys in white clomping past the aisle toward the ice. Steve caught Mark's eye for an instant and then looked past him.

"Hey, Charlie!" he called. "You shouldn't be hanging with the enemy. You're on my side in this war, remember?"

"Yeah, coming," Charlie said, and Mark heard a catch in his voice.

"I'll be waiting." Steve slapped his stick against the lockers, leaving the noise of clanging metal in his wake.

Charlie stared after him and there was the flicker of something like fear in his face.

"You're afraid of him?" Mark said, because that was what it looked like.

"C'mon, get real," Charlie replied, but he had sweat on his upper lip. "Getty can be an ass, but he doesn't scare me." He rubbed a gloved hand across his mouth.

"Are you sure? Did he warn you to keep quiet about something? About Rose?" Mark asked, and jerked the laces on his skates harder than he had to as he finished tying them.

"Why would you say that?" Charlie looked green, like he was about to be sick.

Mark had known the guy since they were eight, when Charlie had been one of the crop of grammar school newbies, teary-eyed and homesick. Mark could read him like a book. "You're lying. You are afraid."

Charlie shook his head. "Let it go—"

"You were there," Mark cut him off. "You were the last one I talked to before I lost it." He got up on his skates so he was eye to eye with Charlie. "I spilled beer on my shoes, I wanted air, but I passed out."

"Everyone was wasted."

"No," Mark insisted. "I was barely even buzzed before Steve handed me a cup from the keg. All of a sudden, I was drooling. You don't think it's crazy that I went down after a few sips? You followed me upstairs, so you must've been worried. Did you see what happened to me? Do you know *anything*?"

Charlie jiggled his stick, glancing up the aisle. "I can't help you, man."

"Can't, or won't?" Mark asked.

Charlie's upper lip got slick again. "Did you tell the cops you were drugged?"

"Yeah."

"Did they buy it?"

Mark shrugged and pulled off his blade guards. He tossed them into his locker before grabbing his gloves and slamming the metal door. "I've got no proof." He looked right into Charlie's face. "Unless someone knows something and isn't saying."

Charlie didn't reply, but his jaw started to twitch.

"C'mon, bro," Mark said, putting a glove on his friend's shoulder and leaning in, lowering his voice. "Don't let me take the fall. Is Getty behind this?"

"You think he killed her?"

"You tell me," Mark replied, and secured the chin strap to his helmet. "Did he get a hard-on when he took that picture of Rose on top of me? Did she tell him to get lost, and he went ape-shit? 'Cause I doubt the dude knows how to take no for an answer."

"Don't do this."

"Do what? Dig for the truth?" Mark kept his eyes on Charlie's, but Charlie looked away.

"If you leave it alone, pretty soon it'll all just go away," Charlie said, and pulled down his grille, covering his face. "Who was that girl anyway? A waitress? She was nothing."

Mark stared at him. "That's not you talking, Charlie. That sounds like Getty." What was going on? Mark's pulse pounded in his veins. If his closest friend wasn't talking, how could he ever find out the truth?

Charlie muttered, "Better head out or Coach will wonder where we are." He started to walk away, but halfway up the aisle, he stopped. "You coming or what?"

"In a sec."

"See you on the ice." Charlie nodded, then shuffled off toward the rink.

Mark slowly got up from the bench, yanking on his gloves and picking up his stick. His shoulders felt tight. His whole body felt tight, full of pent-up frustration and fury so big he wasn't sure what to do with it. Mark had never been thrown under the bus before, not by anyone. He'd always been well liked, admired even. And now . . .

When the going got tough, it was amazing how quickly everyone bailed.

Get your head in the game, he told himself, and plodded along the rubber-matted hallway to the rink. Playing hockey was all he had left. He had to forget about Rose Tatum. Couldn't think about what was in the box sent to Katie, or that prick Getty. He needed to focus on the scrimmage, putting every ounce of his energy into ice time before the upcoming game against Briarcliff.

But hard as he tried, he couldn't do it. He couldn't stop thinking about the party and how wrong it had gone. He'd been on top of the world that Saturday night, wanting to kick back with his teammates and celebrate making it to state.

Now everything had changed. Now his whole world depended on the cops finding a missing girl he barely remembered, on there being some kind of evidence that cleared him. Because he couldn't seem to clear himself.

The coach blew a warning whistle just as Mark pushed out onto the ice and skated around the rink, hugging the boards, getting used to the feel of the stick in his hands, the cold on his skin. He told himself not to look across the red line at Getty, clad in enemy white.

The whistle shrilled again, and Mark forced his thoughts aside, skating to the nearest blue line and settling into a circle with his teammates in black jerseys for shooting drills.

A larger-than-usual crowd filled the stands. Mark couldn't help but wonder if they were there because the team had reached the prep school state championship or out of curiosity because of The Box and the missing girl. He felt like a freak-show attraction. He wondered how many of them had already decided he was guilty. Mark knew of the talk behind his back. It ranged from "he's way too clean-cut to kill anybody" to "he thinks because his dad is headmaster he can get away with anything."

Focus on the ice. Watch the puck, he told himself as he skated to the center, a teammate passing to him from near the net.

He heard a cry from the stands and glanced up. Two boys screamed, "Kill it, Summers! Kill it!" and banged on the Plexiglas. They had the hoods of their Soaring Eagle sweatshirts pulled over their heads, so he could barely see their faces.

"Summers!" someone shouted from nearby, and Mark turned in time to catch the puck on the edge of his stick, whiffing the shot. It wobbled off to the right, bouncing against the skate of a teammate. "Jesus, dude, are you going blind?"

A loud burst of laughter erupted from across the rink, followed by a smothered cry of "Loser!" Mark was sure it came from Getty.

He took another skate around the circle, homing in on the puck that was pushed out to him. Heart pumping, he pulled back his stick and laid into the black disk, sending a fierce slap shot past Charlie and clear into the back of the net. He went around again and again, never missing a shot, until Coach Hart blew the whistle twice, setting the scrimmage in motion.

"Summers and Getty!" the coach called, and gestured that the two should face off in the center of the ice.

Mark skated over, clutching his stick, adrenaline pumping through him. He bent low, the foot of his stick on the ice. Across from him, Steve did the same.

They were eye to eye, staring through the plastic guards on their helmets.

Coach Hart whistled and stepped up as a ref would, prepared to drop the puck, just as Getty said under his breath, "Hey, Summers, when they throw you in jail for hacking up Rose, I'll get to play first line and tap Katie, too."

His pulse pounding in his ears, Mark muttered, "You touch Katie, I'll kill you."

"I'll bet she's wild. Way more than Joelle. The quiet ones always are," Steve said, and laughed.

The coach let the puck go, and Mark dropped his stick and

threw off his gloves, going after Steve. All he felt was fury, all he saw was red heat. He swung at Steve wildly, pounding helmet and pads.

Then Steve's stick hammered his skull and, for an instant, Mark saw bursts of light and then a face that looked like Katie's. She was on top of him, kissing him, and then she was lying on the floor, not moving, and someone was saying, "She's not breathing, dude. She's not breathing."

Was it Steve? Was it *Charlie*?

"Summers!"

Mark shook off the fog as the coach shouted, "Cut the crap!" Hands tugged at him, drawing him up. He steadied himself on his skates, blinked to focus, and spotted Steve smirking.

"Guess you do take after your dad," Getty said. "He couldn't hold on to his woman either. Pussy," he muttered, and spit on the ice.

"You son of a bitch!" Mark hissed, and knocked Steve hard to the ice, sending his helmet flying. Mark kneeled over him, about to punch him in the face when Charlie stepped in.

"Relax, man." Charlie dragged Mark up from the ice, pulling him away.

"You're crazy, you psycho!" he heard Steve shouting before an assistant coach caught his arm and led him away.

Mark was breathing hard, tasted blood in his mouth, and it was still another minute before he could say, "I'm okay, I'm okay." He shook off Charlie's hands and picked up his gloves from the ice.

Coach Hart grabbed Mark's shoulder. "What the hell was

that? You and Getty got a problem, settle it off the ice!" The older man's face was purple as he looked at Mark, nose to nose. "I know you're having a rough time, but you'd better pull it together or you'll be lucky to play this weekend. Hell, we'll all be lucky if we don't have to forfeit. Now get out of here." He let Mark go. "You're done for today."

Mark glanced up at the stands, hardly hearing the noise of the crowd. His gaze flitted over the rows of faces, stopping suddenly when he spotted the dark hair and dark eyes, the down-turned mouth.

It was Katie. And she didn't look happy.

He blinked, and she turned around. He watched her back as she fled through the nearest exit.

Damn, damn, damn.

Mark bent down to retrieve his stick and stared at his own blood on the ice, hating that he'd lost control with Steve again. He had to find a way to remember what had gone down at the party, or he'd never be sure he had nothing to do with Rose's disappearance. And if he couldn't trust himself, how could Katie trust him?

She couldn't, he knew. And in the end, he'd lose her, too.

CHAPTER FIFTEEN

TESSA

"Good morning, Tessa. You're right on time, as usual."

Dr. Capello got up from behind her desk as Tessa entered.

"Please, take a seat," the shrink said, gesturing toward a pair of chairs near a large window that framed a narrow creek and a patch of forest, thick with pines. Her dark eyes followed Tessa as she crossed the office and sat down. "Would you like anything to drink? I've got juice and water."

"I'm fine."

"Great. Then we'll get started."

Tessa unbuttoned her blazer and crossed her feet at the ankles. She reminded herself to relax and keep her face as expressionless as possible. Shrinks could read an awful lot into a frown or the tiniest smile.

"I hope it's been helpful," Dr. Capello said, "coming in weekly again, what with all that's going on."

"Yeah, it has," Tessa said. She knew that was what Dr. Capello wanted to hear. All doctors were the same, it didn't matter what kind. She'd seen enough of them since the fire. When she'd first enrolled in Whitney at eleven, she'd had mandatory sessions with old Dr. Erwin. She'd quickly learned that all she had to do was shed a few tears and he turned into a marshmallow. He'd gone easy on her, never digging too deep. He'd let her ramble about whatever she wanted, while he'd sat attentively, stroking his beard and saying, "Ah, very interesting, my dear." Whenever he'd asked about her childhood, Tessa had avoided discussing the fire. Instead, she'd bring up the orphanage in Russia where she and Peter had been dumped by their birth mom.

She really couldn't remember much about the place. She had been only two when the Lupinskis adopted them. But Peter had filled her in, describing filth and neglect. "I banged my head on crib bars and lay in dirty diapers all day, crying nonstop," she'd confessed to the doc. Peter had given her his share of rice cereal when she was hungry. Peter had wrapped her in his T-shirts when she had soiled her diapers.

After she'd finished her sob story, Dr. Erwin would dab his eyes. "Such a tragic tale!" he'd say. "Quite Dickensian. And look at you now. Once a bud with a broken stem and now a rose full-bloomed," leaving Tessa to feel like she'd scored an A+ on a test.

Unfortunately, Dr. Capello wasn't nearly as easy to impress.

"We've been talking about your friendship with Katie,"

the shrink said. She cocked her head so her dark ponytail fell across one shoulder. "You first met here at Whitney when you were freshman, is that right?"

"Yeah." Tessa nodded, lacing her fingers in her lap. "They stuck us together at Amelia House. We've been roommates ever since."

"Roommates and best friends?"

"Mm-hmm," Tessa agreed.

"You feel a kinship with her, don't you?"

"We're connected, yeah," Tessa said, because it was the truth. "Her dad killed himself, you know. That was hard on Katie. She knows what happened with my parents, how they died in the fire."

"And your brother, too," Dr. Capello added.

"Peter." Tessa said his name even though the shrink already knew it.

"You were seven when they died?"

"I was in second grade." Tessa closed her eyes.

"I know you lived in several foster homes before you came to Whitney on scholarship at eleven."

Tessa sighed. "You obviously know the answers, so why keep asking me about it?" She hated feeling like she was being manipulated. "That doesn't have a thing to do with Katie and me or The Box."

Dr. Capello didn't flinch. "It's just that you seem to relate to Katie so well because you've both suffered terrible losses. That's all. There's no ulterior motive here."

Right. Tessa nearly laughed. But she relaxed, uncurling her fingers from fists. She slid her hands along the arms of the chair. "Katie understands me, and I understand her in a way that no one else does. That no one else ever will."

The shrink pursed her lips. "What about Katie's boyfriend? You don't think he understands her?"

"Mark Summers?" Tessa rolled her eyes. "Katie thinks he does, but I don't see how it's possible. She's not even his type. He dates girls like Joelle Needham who wear too much makeup and carry Zac Posen bags." She plucked at a bit of fuzz on her skirt. "Katie's not superficial like that."

"But Mark is?"

"Yeah," Tessa said, lifting her chin. "Totally."

"Ah," the shrink murmured, and scribbled on her tablet with a stylus. Tessa could hear the faint *tap tap*. "I'll bet it's hard sharing her with someone else, isn't it? Particularly when it's someone you don't like."

Tessa stiffened. "I'm not sure they'll be together much longer. They've almost broken up already. Katie still has time to change her mind about following him to college. He'll probably get a stupid hockey scholarship at an Ivy League school, and she'll end up at the closest community college just to be with him." Tessa got fidgety because just bringing it up ticked her off.

"Oh?" Dr. Capello arched her plucked eyebrows. "So you'd rather she go to the same school as you?"

Tessa smoothed her hands on her skirt. "It'd be nice if we could stay near here. There's a decent enough state university close by. It would be good for everyone, I think."

"Everyone meaning you and Katie?"

Tessa shrugged.

"I'm curious," Dr. Capello said, and tapped the stylus against her chin. "Did you know Mark before? When you started at Whitney, I mean. His father was headmaster by then, and you're the same age. It's a pretty small school."

"Everyone knows him." Tessa clasped her hands in her lap. "He'd be kind of hard to miss."

"Did he ever do something to hurt you, like tease you or bully you?"

"You make it sound so simple." Tessa gave her a funny look. She couldn't help it. "I could lie and tell you he called me names and tortured me. But he didn't."

"Then why do you dislike him?" Dr. Capello crossed her legs, leaning forward. "He seems popular enough. Homecoming king, captain of the hockey club."

"Do I have to like him just because other people do?"

"No. But there's usually a reason for disliking someone. A history."

Tessa hesitated. "It's not just him, it's everyone like him. They don't appreciate what they have," she finally said. "Mark has a father who goes out of his way to protect him, and he takes advantage of that, like having that party while his dad was away."

"So that makes him unlikable?"

Wasn't that a good enough reason? Tessa sighed, taking it further. "He cheated on Katie! *That* makes him unlikable."

"But Katie doesn't agree?"

Tessa frowned. "Katie was lucky to find out who he really is before it was too late. If he did something to that girl, Rose, who's to say Katie wouldn't be next?"

"You think he's violent?"

"Have you ever watched him play hockey?"

"It's a rough sport," Dr. Capello said. "But it's not real life."

Tessa snorted. "Maybe you should go to the rink sometime. You might change your mind."

Dr. Capello stared at her for a long, uncomfortable moment, then glanced down, scribbling on her tablet again. "So Mark isn't the right guy for Katie?"

"He's not like us," Tessa said, scooting to the edge of her seat, wishing the shrink would see her point. It wasn't like it was so complicated. "He's been given everything on a silver platter. If you haven't ever gone through something horrible, you can't appreciate when you've got someone special in your life."

"His father raised him alone," the shrink said, and Tessa nodded—it was something everyone at Whitney knew. "In a way, he lost a parent, too."

"Please." Tessa wanted to scream. "His mother's not dead, is she? She just ran off with some guy. Mark could see her if he wanted to. It's not like he had to stand outside his own house and watch it burn, knowing who was trapped inside and not being able to do anything about it."

Tessa clamped her mouth shut. She'd said too much already.

Dr. Capello set aside her tablet. "Would you like to—"

"Talk about it?" Tessa felt like she'd explode if anyone asked her that again. "No, thanks," she said coolly. She jumped up from the chair and walked to the big window. "Are we done?" she asked, and gazed out to the woods, where a bunch of men had gathered. Two of them were holding dogs that strained on their leads. "I should really go find Katie. She's not taking things well. Life can be rough on sensitive girls."

"Life can be rough on everyone."

Tessa kept staring out the window. "Does it ever make you numb, Dr. Capello, hearing everyone's problems day after day after day?"

"When people feel broken, sometimes they feel ignored, too. They just need someone to hear them. I do my best to listen."

"What if they're too broken to fix?" Tessa asked, touching her fingertips to the glass. "What do you do with them then?"

"I try to help them change."

"What if it's too late to do anything at all?" Tessa asked, staring outside, watching the men and the dogs weave through the trees, making circles, their movements increasingly frantic. "What if they can't change? What if they're so screwed up they're more like ghosts of themselves than real people?"

She saw Dr. Capello's reflection in the glass as the shrink came up behind her.

"Are you sure there isn't anything I can do for you, Tessa? Don't be afraid to ask for help. It doesn't mean you're weak."

"Anything you can do for *me*?" Tessa turned around. She

made a noise of disbelief. "You think I was talking about myself?"

"I don't know," the woman said, looking her in the eye. "Were you?"

"No, Dr. Capello, I wasn't talking about myself." Tessa's hands started shaking. "Unlike the majority of self-absorbed snobs at Whitney Prep, everything I say isn't always about me."

Then, without another word, she left.

CHAPTER SIXTEEN

KATIE

After her first class, Katie waited for Tessa outside the administration building. She knew Tessa had a Wednesday-morning session with Dr. Capello, and Tessa rarely missed classes or mandatory counseling. Her scholarship depended on it.

Katie hadn't seen her since the night before. Tessa still wasn't in bed at four a.m. when Katie got back from the greenhouse with Mark. She hadn't returned to their room by the time Katie had to dress and leave. Where had Tessa gone and what was going on with her? Why was her best friend keeping secrets?

When Katie saw Tessa's pale hair glinting in the sunlight, she waved her down. "We need to talk," she said.

"What's with the sour face?" Tessa asked. She had her thumbs looped in the straps of her backpack. "You look like you OD'd on toxic waste."

"No more games, Tessa," Katie said, too tired for verbal sparring. "Just tell me where you went, okay?"

"What do you mean, where I went?" Tessa replied. "I was getting grilled by the school shrink, like every Wednesday. She had me trapped in her office for an hour. Now you're in my face, too? Jeez." She shook her head and started walking.

"That's not what I meant." Katie hurried to keep up. "Where'd you go last night? I woke up from one of my freaky dreams, and you were standing by my bed." Katie had glimpsed Tessa's pale skin and pale hair. Who else could it have been? "Then you ran out of the room, and I found a rose petal on the floor—"

"What?" Tessa stopped walking and gave her a funny look. "That's bananas."

"Have you been watching me at night, Tessa?" Katie asked, because she couldn't help wondering. "Are you trying to psych me out or something?"

"You think I'm the ghost from your dream? You're joking, right?"

But Katie was dead serious. "You're hiding something."

"And you must be *on* something," Tessa shot back, "because you're totally imagining things. I couldn't sleep, so I went down to the basement to watch TV again. That's all."

"You were in the basement?"

"There was a *Real World* marathon, so I tuned in until I fell asleep," Tessa said, so easily that Katie might have believed her.

Except she knew it was a lie.

Katie stared at her friend, her heart aching. There was no question in her mind that Tessa was covering something up.

"What's with the third degree?" Tessa turned aside as a group of students brushed past. "You weren't in bed when I came back upstairs. So maybe I should ask where you were, and please, don't tell me you snuck out with Mark again."

"I wouldn't have run into him if I hadn't been looking for you, and thank God I did or I'd still be stuck in the tunnels," Katie said without thinking.

Tessa turned red. "You *did* see him, Katie! What's wrong with you?"

"What's wrong with *you*? You're avoiding my question," Katie said. "Where'd you go, Tessa?"

Why did they always go in circles? Why wasn't Tessa coming clean? Why was her friend turning this around on her? Katie was getting such weird vibes she didn't know what to do. She opened her mouth to say, "Just tell me what you were doing in the steam tunnels and why you ran away from me," when a scream stopped her cold.

"They found her!" someone yelled from farther up the sidewalk. Suddenly, she heard the dogs, howling so loudly the air practically vibrated around them.

Had the search dogs tracked Rose?

Katie glanced ahead, squinting, and grabbed Tessa's arm. "Oh, my God," she said, and her stomach did a nervous flutter. "Let's go." She flung her book bag over her shoulder and started running, following a crowd of people.

Katie felt like a wildebeest merging in with a migrating

herd as she raced across campus. Elbows, feet, and book bags swung this way and that, bumping into her as the herd cut through neatly trimmed lawns between the stone buildings, then rushed down the gently sloping hill toward the creek.

"Hey, wait up!" she heard Tessa call from behind her, but she didn't slow down.

Her breath came hard and fast as she ran toward the greenhouse and the maintenance shed. Then the forward motion of the students slowed and ground to a halt.

"Excuse me, sorry," Katie said, pushing her way through until she found the cause: the campus police were setting up sawhorse barricades on the near side of the creek so no one could cross.

"Stay back, please, stay back," they kept saying, doing their best to keep the students a safe distance from the woods.

"Is it true, they found the missing girl?" a girl asked the campus cops.

The cops looked at each other but didn't answer.

Katie strained to see what was going on not more than thirty yards away. The braying of the dogs went on, rattling her eardrums. She watched one of them, a reddish-colored bloodhound, pulling hard against the leash held by a police officer.

"Bring the shovels!" a deep voice bellowed from the woods.

"They must've found something," the girl beside Katie murmured, "or else why would they be digging?"

Katie's book bag felt heavy, the strap biting into her shoulder. Then someone jostled her from behind, and her bag slid down her arm to the ground. She reached for it, and when she stood, she saw Mark, edging into a spot beside her.

"Hey," she said, staring up at him.

He had a nasty bruise on his forehead. She didn't need to ask what had happened. She'd gone to hockey practice before first period; sitting high in the stands, her gaze was on Mark as he skated. He'd seemed off during warm-ups, out of his usual rhythm and out of sync with the rest of his teammates. Then he'd gone after Steve Getty again, and Katie had found it too ugly to watch.

She'd left the rink as fast as she could.

I would never hurt you, Mark had texted her soon after.

You are hurting yourself, she typed back. Don't let him get to you.

If Mark wanted to convince everyone that he was innocent, he had to stop lashing out at Steve. It just made him look angry and unpredictable and capable of anything.

"What are you doing here?" Katie asked when Mark didn't say anything. It wasn't wise for him to be hanging around the woods where the dogs were searching, when the police thought he was the last one to see Rose alive.

"I have to know if it's her," he said, and snatched Katie's bag from the ground.

Without another word, he headed through the crowd of students, away from the barricades, and toward a thick copse of trees in the opposite direction.

"Mark, don't," Katie said, following him. She heard Tessa call her name. But she didn't turn around.

"C'mon, stop," she said, but he kept on walking. If he didn't have her book bag, she would have let him go. But instead she hurried after him as he pushed his way through overgrown bushes that scratched Katie's hands and face. The crowded trees with their thick green canopies shut out the sun. Katie sidestepped tangled roots, twigs, and pine cones. She tripped and caught herself on a tree dark with sap. Her palm came away sticky.

"Please, stop," she said again, but he just kept going.

He followed some path that Katie couldn't see until she heard the dogs again and voices, and she realized what they'd done. They'd gone the long way around and come up behind the cops.

Mark paused and turned, putting a finger to his lips. He set her bag down quietly and took her hand. They crept forward and crouched behind a messy tangle of wild honeysuckle. Mark parted the branches enough that they could see the dozen police officers and campus security loosely circling a spot where men with shovels were attacking the earth.

No one spoke for what seemed an eternity. There was just the scuffling of the dogs, the labored breath of those digging, and the spades hitting dirt.

Brush and stones had been cleared from the spot. The dug-up dirt looked different, lighter and softer, like freshly ground coffee.

Mark didn't move. He didn't look at her. His gaze was fixed dead ahead. He was so still Katie wondered if he was holding his breath. She wasn't sure how much time elapsed before one noisy *clunk* rang out, and then another, as shovels struck stone.

"Careful now," a man called out, and Katie recognized the detective who'd questioned her at Amelia House. "Let's get those rocks out by hand."

The men tossed their shovels aside and dropped to their knees, drawing out flattened stones from the creek, setting them aside with gloved hands.

"Must've laid them over her so the critters wouldn't get her," one of the cops said loudly enough for them to hear.

Critters? Ugh.

Katie looked at Mark. He still held her hand, and his skin felt ice-cold.

"Okay, let's take it slow," the detective said. "Anything that's not dirt or twigs, I want bagged. And make sure we get photographs every step of the way."

Katie caught a glimpse of white against the earth.

"Is it her?" she whispered. "Is that Rose?"

But Mark didn't answer.

She bit her lip, waiting, as endless minutes ticked past.

"Use the brushes now and sift the dirt nice and easy. Let's not miss a hair," the detective said, and then he disappeared from Katie's view as one of the officers shifted position, blocking her line of sight with his shoulders.

"I can't see," Mark said under his breath

But Katie didn't want to see, not really. If it was Rose, what would she look like? Pale and waxen like Mr. Ogden? Probably worse, if she'd been in the ground since she'd gone missing over a week ago. Was her skull full of maggots, wiggling in and out of her eye sockets?

Katie tasted bile and swallowed hard.

Mark moved to the left and peeked through the branches. He sighed, looking grim, and Katie knew he could see again.

She didn't want to look. So she stared at her shoes. Her black flats were wet and caked with mud. They were as good as ruined.

"Aw, hell," Mark said, and Katie had to peek.

She settled in beside Mark and gazed through the thick honeysuckle. Now there was no one in the way, nothing to obstruct the view. What Katie saw poking out of the shallow grave was a face—or what was left of one—discolored and gray. It looked like a Halloween mask, not a person. The men kept brushing away bits of earth that covered the corpse like a blanket until something around its throat glinted in the dappled light: a gold chain with a charm.

Katie's breath caught. Was that the St. Sebastian medal she'd given Mark?

One of the cops held up the chain so another could bag it, and Katie saw enough to feel sure that's what it was. Mark hadn't just lost the medallion the night of the party; somehow it had ended up with Rose Tatum. Had she stolen it from him? Had he given it to her? Could he really not know where it had gone?

"Mark?" she said, so quietly she wasn't sure he heard. And then he looked at her with such wide eyes that she knew he'd seen it, too.

"I swear—" he started to say, and Katie shook her head. She didn't want to hear another denial. She couldn't stomach it.

What had happened two weekends ago on that Saturday night that Rose went missing? Who had killed her and buried her across the creek in the woods? What if Mark wasn't telling the truth? What if he *could* remember and the rest was a lie told to cover up the bad things he'd done?

Don't go there, she told herself. But it was too late. She'd already gone.

Katie closed her eyes. She drew away from Mark, dizzy and nauseated.

Rose Tatum had finally turned up.

And she was very, very dead.

CHAPTER SEVENTEEN

KATIE

It took hours for the cops to unearth and remove Rose's remains.

Katie didn't stick around to watch. Glimpsing what was left of Rose Tatum had made her sick. She wished she hadn't gone into the woods with Mark to watch them dig. What had happened to Rose was real. It wasn't a joke. A girl was dead, and whoever had murdered her could still be lurking around campus.

When she'd seen enough, Katie had grabbed her book bag from Mark and fled the woods. She wasn't even aware that he'd followed until he caught up to her near the creek. When he touched her, Katie flinched, and she saw the hurt in his eyes as he let his hand fall away.

"I didn't do it," he said, but it sounded so hollow this time. Like even he wasn't sure he believed it.

"How'd she get your medallion?" Katie asked. "If you had nothing to do with her, why was she wearing it?"

"I don't know."

Katie felt like screaming. "You have to do better than that. You *have* to remember! I've seen a dozen Lifetime movies where people get hypnotized and recover lost memories. Maybe you should try that. You have to do *something*. We'll never know what really happened that night if you keep drawing a blank!"

Mark flinched. His bruised face looked so pained. "At least she's not missing anymore," he said grimly. "We know that much now, don't we?"

Then he walked off, and Katie stood there for a long time, staring down at her muddy shoes.

Was finding Rose really a good thing? She had a sinking feeling that the cops were going to drag Mark back in for another round of questioning. What if they arrested him this time and threw him in jail? What if they stopped looking for anyone else? What if they didn't *need* to keep looking?

The whole world felt totally scrambled.

It was like one of those awful thousand-piece jigsaw puzzles her dad had loved putting together. "Bonding time," he'd called it, but for Katie it felt more like torture. Often they'd spent a whole weekend on a single puzzle. They would find the border pieces first and then move inward, doing small portions until those connected into something bigger. And when they'd finally stuck in that last piece (which had usually fallen to the floor and required a search on hands and knees), her dad would always say, "Whoever thought all those tiny bits of nothing would end up looking like *that*?" *That* being a truly dazzling photograph of a rain forest or the Taj Mahal or a villa in Tuscany.

Only Katie didn't have all the pieces to the puzzle yet. She couldn't even find the borders. So how was she supposed to figure out the whole picture?

Leave it to the police, it's their job, a tiny voice instructed. But Katie didn't like feeling helpless. She had to do *something*. If she focused on small things, things she could do, that would be a start.

First, she had to deal with her unfinished business with Tessa.

She looked for her roommate, but Tessa wasn't anywhere near the barricades. By then, only a few dozen students remained. Katie's gaze drifted away from the creek toward the greenhouse, and she saw a solitary boy staring in her direction. He had his hands in his jacket pockets, the collar turned up. He gave her a long, hard look before he turned and headed off.

Steve Getty.

Katie shivered, staring at his retreating back. Had he really drugged Mark the night of the party? Had he done something to Rose? Or was it just that he was such an ass it made him easy to blame?

"I know what you're thinking," a voice said from behind her. "But if you're going after Steve, you'd better be careful."

Katie turned to find Joelle Needham standing a few feet away.

"He may act like an obnoxious puppy, but he's the wolf that ate Red Riding Hood's grandma."

What did Joelle think she was going to do? Run after Steve and accuse him of murder in front of everyone on campus?

"I wasn't going to—" Katie started to say.

"Snoop around?" Joelle finished for her. "So you don't want to clear Mark?"

Katie pursed her lips. Of course she wanted proof that Mark was innocent! She wanted that more than anything. "I just want to find the truth," she said.

"Ah, the truth." Joelle came closer, and Katie saw what looked like a bruise on her jaw beneath her carefully applied concealer. "Some people around here will do anything to keep the truth from getting out."

"Joelle, if you know something—if Steve hurt you—you need to talk," Katie said. "You should tell the headmaster. If no one ever speaks, he'll keep doing it. Maybe not at Whitney but at whatever college he goes to—"

"I can't," Joelle cut her off. "I just can't."

Katie glanced at the mark on Joelle's jaw. "Did he hit you?"

Joelle touched the spot and shook her head. "I was attacked by my blow-dryer," she said. "Really," she added when Katie squinted at her. "I swear to God, if Steve hit me, I'd hit him back."

Then what was holding her back? Katie wondered. Did Steve have pictures or video? "Is he blackmailing you?"

Joelle clammed up.

"You can't let it go." Katie's dad had kept a big secret about losing all their money and then he'd killed himself because of it. "Some secrets need to be told."

"Not this one. Not by me," Joelle said, and blindly bumped into Katie as she hurried past.

Katie held her arm like she'd been stung. What had just happened? Joelle was warning her off Steve? Why did Mark's ex care what she did? Joelle didn't even like her. Everyone was acting so bizarre. She thought of a poem by Emily Dickinson that she'd had to memorize this semester:

> *Much Madness is divinest Sense*
> *To a discerning Eye*
> *Much Sense — the starkest Madness —*
> *'Tis the Majority*
> *In this, as all, prevail —*
> *Assent — and you are sane —*
> *Demur — you're straightaway dangerous —*
> *And handled with a Chain —*

If you thought you were mad, then you were probably sane. If you thought you were sane and everyone agreed, you probably weren't. And if you stood up for yourself against the crowd, you were dangerous.

Katie definitely felt like she was losing it these days. She hoped that meant she wasn't really nuts, at least according to Emily.

With a sigh, she started up the hill toward campus. On the way, she reached for her phone to text Tessa where r u, and something fell out of her pocket. A folded slip of paper settled on the grass. She stopped and picked it up. Two lines were printed across the sheet:

PHILLIPS EXETER, PHILLIPS ANDOVER, ST. PAUL'S, WESTMINSTER. WHAT DO THEY ALL HAVE IN COMMON?

Had Joelle stuck the paper in Katie's pocket when she'd bumped into her? Was Mark's ex actually trying to help? The four names on the list were all private prep schools, Katie knew, very much like Whitney.

He may act like an obnoxious puppy, but he's the wolf that ate Red Riding Hood's grandma.

Had Steve Getty gone to Phillips Exeter, Phillips Andover, St. Paul's, and Westminster before Whitney? Katie had heard that Whitney was the fifth school he'd attended, so that would fit. Why had Steve transferred in the middle of his senior year? That wasn't normal. Nobody wanted to switch schools so close to graduation. Had he done something awful that made the four other schools kick him out?

Maybe Joelle wasn't talking outright, but she was talking. Katie didn't know exactly what had happened between Joelle and Steve, but she was certain of one thing: Steve Getty was involved in this mess with Rose Tatum up to his eyeballs. He'd known her before the party. He'd snuck her onto campus and used her in those pictures with Mark. Katie felt sure he had something to do with her disappearance. Maybe he'd even killed her.

Katie had tried Googling Steve's name and had only found interviews with his ambassador dad or hockey stats. Nothing about why he couldn't seem to stay put. If Katie was going to learn anything more, she had to look at Steve's academic records. Or at least get someone to look at them for her.

Bea Lively volunteered in the Student Affairs Office, mostly working with leaders of various groups on campus. She'd helped set up the poetry slam in January, which was when they'd gotten to be friends. If anyone could take a peek at a student's records without hacking, it would be Bea. Katie figured it was worth a shot.

So she headed straight for the administration building and Student Affairs. When she walked through the door, the phones were trilling, and a pair of gray-haired women behind the counter seemed to be scrambling to keep up. They didn't even glance at Katie when she approached. But Katie didn't need them.

"Bea?"

A tall girl with bright orange braids hanging down the back of her burgundy blazer was putting up event notices on the bulletin board. Bea turned her freckled face toward Katie. "Hey," she said, giving a little wave. She had a wrist full of handmade bracelets, yellow tights under her burgundy-and-black plaid skirt, and brown clogs. Bea was not a slave to fashion.

"Have you got a sec?" Katie asked.

"Hang on, okay?" Bea finished pressing pushpins into a flyer, then walked over to Katie. "How're you doing? I heard they found that missing girl. The phones are going bonkers. I had to take a break."

"That's kind of why I'm here." Katie looked over at the women behind the counter. They were busy answering calls and didn't seem to be listening, but Katie didn't want to take any chances. She drew Bea toward a pair of chairs against the far wall.

Above them, a framed poster of a broadly smiling girl and boy hovered. Bold black letters screamed WHITNEY ACADEMY IS THE PLACE TO BE!

Yeah, Katie thought, it was the place to be if you liked sharing the campus with a psycho killer.

"What's up?" Bea asked. "You're not here to get your transcript forwarded, are you? I know your mom wants you to leave, but they'll catch the guy soon, I'm sure they will, and graduation's coming up so fast."

"I'm not leaving."

"Phew."

"I need you to do something for me."

"You look so serious." Bea wrinkled her forehead. "So is the favor illegal or immoral?"

"A little of both," Katie said, and wet her lips. "Can you look at someone's records for me?"

"Like, their grades?"

Katie shook her head. "Like why they left their other schools."

"Who are we talking about?" Bea pulled a braid forward and twisted it.

Katie kept her voice low. "Steve Getty."

Bea dropped the braid. "The ambassador's son?"

"Yeah."

"What'd he do? Besides thinking he's God's gift to women, I mean."

Katie didn't know a way to put it nicely. "I think he might have date-raped someone."

"For real?" Bea looked horrified. "Why would Whitney let him in if they knew? Screw that"—she waved a hand in the air—"why isn't he in jail?"

"Maybe the school didn't know. Maybe Steve's dad kept everyone quiet," Katie replied, thinking of something Tessa had said.

People get away with stuff all the time around here. And if their parents can't buy them out of it, they just yank them from school and they start all over again somewhere else.

Steve Getty's dad was high-profile enough to pull plenty of strings and quietly pass out hush money.

"I'm toast if I get caught, but I'll do my best," Bea said, and her gaze shifted toward the women behind the counter. "Student volunteers aren't supposed to handle transcripts. But if the phones keep ringing nonstop, I can probably get to the computer in back for a few minutes alone."

"Please try," Katie begged. Her phone buzzed, but she ignored it. "I think Steve might have had something to do with Rose Tatum."

"The dead girl?" Bea said, and got quiet for a moment. "But everyone's saying Mark was the last one—"

"I know what they're saying," Katie cut her off. She'd begun having doubts of her own, and it sickened her. "What if everyone's wrong?"

Bea's eyes filled with pity. "But, Katie, what if they're right?"

"Call me if you find out anything," she said, and grabbed her book bag.

As Katie walked out the door, her phone buzzed again. She left it in her pocket till she was outside. She took a deep breath of spring air and glanced around from the top of the building steps. A police cruiser rolled slowly past and then another. Her pulse picked up. She couldn't help wondering if they were going to arrest Mark.

A couple of students walked by, staring at her, and Katie scooted over to a pillar, tucking her shoulder against the column to check her messages. The most recent two were from Tessa, and the words nearly made Katie's heart stop:

You're right. I have a secret, the first text said. And the second, Come to dr c's now & I will tell you all I know.

CHAPTER EIGHTEEN

MARK

It didn't take long for the police to come calling after Rose was found.

They caught Mark at home between classes. No more playing nice and asking for cooperation. They had a warrant this time, signed by a county judge. They wanted to search several rooms at the headmaster's house and Mark's locker at the ice rink.

While the housekeeper kept them in the foyer, Mark called his dad, who arrived minutes after with the school's general counsel. The lawyer looked over the paperwork and gave a grim nod. Mark's father frowned.

"If you just tell us what you want, we'll get it for you," he told the police captain, but the officer asked him to stay back and let them do their job.

"You should get to class," his dad suggested, but Mark couldn't go.

His stomach was doing flip-flops. How could he leave when they were digging through his stuff? What were they looking for exactly? If they wanted to find strands of Rose's hair or her fingerprints, they probably would. She was here at the party—no one was denying that fact.

Charlie had helped Mark clean up afterward, tossing sticky cups and mopping up puddles of beer. Mark hadn't seen blood anywhere. Not a drop.

He stood aside, watching as they worked their way through the house. First, they focused on the basement rec room, then Mark's bedroom and the maid's room, where Mark had told them he'd passed out.

They rifled through drawers, tossed sofa cushions, and even asked his dad for the key to the liquor cabinet. A uniform wearing latex gloves and booties vacuumed lint from the rugs. They dusted doorknobs for prints and took the linens from the beds along with a pair of Mark's shoes and his hairbrush. Everything got packed into big brown bags that were tagged and taken out to a waiting police car.

Annalisa moaned at the mess they left behind, and Mark's dad didn't seem any too happy about it, either.

"For God's sake, this is my home, not a crime scene," his father muttered to the lawyer, and then Mark overheard them talking about the cops issuing a warrant for the greenhouse, too. They wanted to confiscate pruning saws and shovels.

Did they think Mark had killed Rose, then used a saw from the greenhouse to cut off her hand and a shovel to bury her? They'd already fingerprinted him and taken a sample of his DNA. Was it just a matter of time before they cuffed him and hauled him off?

I'm sorry, he wanted to tell his dad again. Because all of this was his fault. He'd brought this on, even if he hadn't meant to. And it wasn't going away.

Before the cops had finished, when no one was paying him any attention, Mark skipped out. He took off on his bike, heading to the rink as fast as he could pedal. If they were going to paw through his locker next, he wanted to get there first.

He tried to remember what was in there. Dirty socks. Jockstraps. Helmet. Skates. Extra blades. Nothing that his teammates wouldn't have. Nothing worth shit to anyone but him. Definitely nothing to do with that girl.

But when he got to the rink, there was a black and white Barnard police car sitting out front. Another one? Were they executing the search warrants all at once?

Breathing hard, Mark pedaled around back, dropping his bike to the grass and rushing in through the rear door.

He saw Steve and Charlie and a few other guys hanging around the coach's office. "Dude," he heard Steve mutter, "you're in big trouble."

Mark silently walked past. He wasn't going to be baited into a fight this time.

"Hey, Summers, they said to keep back," Charlie told him, but Mark didn't listen.

He went around the rows of lockers, turning into the aisle where his locker was. "Um, excuse me," he said to the two cops picking through his stuff, "but that's my locker."

"You're Mark Summers?"

"Yeah."

A uniform stopped him before he got too close, but he could see that the locker door was wide open. They hadn't needed to crowbar it. His lock had been broken for ages. Mark hadn't cared. He'd never kept anything valuable in there. He couldn't imagine anyone ever wanting to lift a bunch of sweaty nut cups.

"Just give us some room," the officer said. "It won't be long."

Mark nodded, moving toward the end of the aisle.

They'd tossed aside most of his stuff except for a towel brown with dried blood—*his* blood, he was sure—which was quickly stuffed into an evidence bag.

Then one of the cops held something in his latex-gloved hand. "Looks like a burner," he said, his gaze shifting toward Mark.

The other nodded. "Bag it."

"That's not mine," Mark told them, because it wasn't. He had his phone in his back pocket, and the one they removed from his locker looked like a crappy flip phone. *A burner,* the cop had said. The prepaid kind you used when you couldn't afford a contract, Mark thought. The kind that kept your calls anonymous. Only he'd never seen this one before. "I don't know how it got there," he told them.

But he had a horrible feeling he knew whose it was.

CHAPTER NINETEEN

TESSA

Tessa's eyes watched the clock. Was Katie coming or not?

"I can stay about another twenty minutes, but that's all," Dr. Capello said from behind her desk. "Then I've got to head to my office in town. Do you want to talk about whatever it is now? Is it so important that Katie be here, too?"

"Yeah," Tessa told her, staring at the door, "it is."

She'll show, Tessa thought. *She has to.*

Another five minutes ticked past and then the door flew open.

Katie poked her head in, and Tessa jumped up from her chair, walking toward her. "You came," she said. "I knew you would."

"What's up with you?" Katie whispered, looking past Tessa's shoulder at the school shrink. "Why'd you want to meet me here? Why not back at the dorm?"

"Dr. C should hear this, too," Tessa told her. She needed someone else in the room, someone who might actually believe her.

"Have a seat, Katie." Dr. Capello gestured to the chairs near her desk. "Let's hear what Tessa has to say."

Despite her skeptical expression, Katie sat and placed her book bag on the floor by her feet. She pushed her long hair behind her ears, then settled back. "Okay," she said, "I'm listening."

Tessa's armpits felt damp. She was nervous, even though she'd been gearing up for this for days. "I haven't been straight with you," she said, and forced herself to meet Katie's eyes. "I didn't mean to keep secrets, but I was scared. I wasn't sure what to do, but then they found the girl, and I knew I couldn't stay quiet—"

"Tessa, just *spill*," Katie said, sounding tired. She looked tired, too. There were gray shadows beneath her eyes.

Tessa wet her lips. "I know something about the night Rose Tatum disappeared, more than I've told you. Something Mark can't seem to remember."

"Oh, my God." Katie threw up her hands. "This is about bashing Mark? Been there, done that. Sorry, Dr. Capello, but I'm out of here." She grabbed her bag and headed toward the door.

"I promised him I wouldn't tell," Tessa blurted out. She couldn't let Katie leave. She had to listen! "He was totally trashed when he called me that night."

Katie stopped and turned around.

Tessa swallowed. Her mouth was bone dry. "I thought he'd dialed me by mistake. He was rambling so badly I could hardly understand him. He said there was an accident . . . that she wasn't breathing."

"What are you talking about?" Katie took a step toward her. "Who drunk-dialed you? You can't mean Mark?"

"Yeah," Tessa said. "I mean Mark."

Katie let her bag slide to the floor with a thump. "Liar," she said, with such force it felt like a knife in Tessa's heart. "Mark wouldn't call you if he was dying and you were the last person left on earth."

"He was desperate."

"He'd never be *that* desperate." Katie exhaled loudly. "What a story, Tessa!" She shook her head. "How long did it take you to make it up? Almost two weeks, I guess, since Rose disappeared."

"He made me swear I wouldn't tell!" Tessa couldn't give up. Katie had to understand. "He threatened to have me expelled!"

"Liar," Katie said again.

"I'm not." Tessa squished her eyes closed, the words echoing inside her head. *You're a liar!* their adopted mother had shouted at Peter whenever he'd denied stealing from her purse or breaking something. Even when he hadn't done it—even when Tessa was the guilty one—he took the brunt of it. They were always yelling at him or arguing about him. *He's too damaged,* she'd heard their mother crying behind their parents' closed bedroom door at night. *Something's wrong with him. I can't control him. He's a ticking time bomb.*

146

"Please, Tessa, go on," Dr. Capello said in that sooth-ing voice that always tried to get Tessa to say more than she wanted. "I'd like to hear the rest."

Tessa opened her eyes and focused on the shrink. She couldn't look at Katie yet.

"Okay," she said, and swallowed again. She knew what had happened that night. She could recite every detail. She'd gone over it a thousand times in her head. "I started over to the headmaster's house but I chickened out. I couldn't do it. I tried to pretend nothing had happened. I didn't want to believe he'd really done it, until they found her in the woods. I thought he was too drunk that night to know what he was saying."

"Have I got this right?" Katie said, and began ticking off points on her fingers. "Mark killed Rose, then called you for help. And when you didn't show, he cut off her hand, dropped it off for me at Amelia House, and buried her in the woods. Did I leave anything out? Like maybe you ran into aliens or morphed into a werewolf?"

"Don't do that," Tessa said, hating the way Katie stared at her with such disappointment, as though she didn't like her, much less trust her. "I don't know why Mark did what he did. I'm not a shrink. But all those things happened, whether or not you want to believe me."

Katie's eyes turned bright with tears. "Then why didn't you say something before now? Why did you wait so long? It doesn't make sense, Tessa. None of this makes sense."

"I didn't want to hurt you!" Tessa cried out, wondering why Katie couldn't see that by now. It was so obvious. "All

I've been trying to do is look out for you! Since the day we met, that's all I've done."

"Look out for me? Is that what you call what you've been doing?" Katie's voice shook. "I think you want to scare me, Tessa. Things haven't been right since I started seeing Mark. That's when I started having the bad dreams. That's when I started feeling like someone was watching me. When maybe it was you all along."

"No."

"So you didn't sneak into the library stacks and set a rose on my bag during midterms?"

"No," Tessa said.

"How do I know you're not standing over me while I sleep, saying my name?" Katie went on, like she didn't believe her. "Did you watch me while I slept last night? Did you have a rose in the room? I found a petal—"

"No!" Tessa bristled.

"I saw your pale hair, I saw your pale skin." Tears began to skid down Katie's cheeks. "It was you, Tessa. Who else could it have been?"

"It wasn't me!" Tessa clenched her hands into fists.

Katie brushed at her cheeks and said nothing.

Tessa could hardly breathe.

"Ladies, let's take this down a notch, okay?" Dr. Capello interjected. She got up from her desk and put a hand on Tessa's shoulder. "It's been a very tense couple of weeks," she said. "Sometimes it's easy for people to confuse reality and subconscious desires when they're under a lot of stress—"

"I'm not confused," Tessa said, pulling away from her. "Everything I told you did happen."

"Give me your phone," Katie said through her tears, holding out her hand. "If Mark called you that Saturday night, his number will show up."

Tessa shook her head. "He didn't use his own phone," she said. "The number came up anonymous, like those disposable phones you buy at Walmart. I think it was the dead girl's."

"Do you see what I mean?" Katie turned to Dr. Capello. "She's making this up! When it comes to Mark, she'll say anything."

"If the police have found Rose Tatum's phone, they'll know if a call was placed to Tessa," the school shrink said, like she was the voice of reason. "They'll check it for evidence."

Tessa rubbed damp palms on her skirt.

"But can anyone prove that it was Mark who called her?" Katie asked. "What if it was someone else?"

"Who else do you think it was?" Tessa asked. "Rose was already dead."

"Why are you doing this, Tessa?" Katie asked, the tears coming faster now. She wiped her sleeve against her nose. "Are you trying to make things even worse?"

"No." Tessa shook her head. "I'm trying to make them better."

"Better for you?" Katie murmured. "This is so messed up—*you're* messed up." Then she snatched her book bag and ran out of the room. The door slammed, and she was gone.

Tessa shut her eyes, gritting her teeth as Dr. Capello rattled on. "I have to call the headmaster," she was saying, and picked up the phone, "and I'm sure you'll have to tell your story to the police, too. . . ."

You're messed up, messed up, messed up.

Why couldn't Katie just accept that Mark was no good for her? Then she could stop wasting time on someone who didn't really love her and move on with her life.

"I really wish you'd let me help you," Dr. Capello said, not for the first time.

Tessa sat there, still as stone. She didn't need help from the shrink. The only other person she'd ever been able to truly count on besides herself was her brother. She wished Peter could swoop in and rescue her now. But Tessa knew she was on her own.

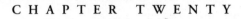

CHAPTER TWENTY

KATIE

Katie ran out of the building, not sure what to do next. Tessa's sudden confession was beyond surreal, worse than any nightmare. How many times in the last four years had Katie turned to Tessa when something went wrong? And then she'd begun to count on Mark as much as Tessa, maybe more. But now Katie didn't know who or what to believe. She felt completely lost. Where was she supposed to go when she wasn't sure who to trust anymore?

Katie didn't go far. She ended up on a bench across from the building, sitting in the shadow of a giant oak. Brushing tears from her cheeks, she watched students walk past and tried to remember how it felt when her only fear was an upcoming exam, not whether or not her best friend was a pathological liar and her boyfriend a murderer.

A campus cop car pulled up in front of the administration

offices. The chief of campus security got out from the driver's side just before Dr. Capello emerged from the building, escorting Tessa down the steps.

Katie got up and stood beneath the shade of the tree, staring as Tessa climbed into the car. The security chief exchanged a few words with Dr. Capello before he got behind the wheel and drove off. The school shrink lingered a moment before she turned and headed toward the faculty parking lot.

Instinctively, Katie grabbed her bag and ran after her.

"Dr. Capello, wait up!" she called, reaching the lot just as the psychiatrist tossed a leather case onto the passenger seat of her Volvo.

Dr. Capello shut the door and straightened. "Katie?"

"I need to talk about Tessa. She's seriously messed up."

"I know you're concerned," Dr. Capello said as she rounded the car to the driver's-side door. "But we have to let the police take over from here. It's out of my hands. If Tessa's making things up, they'll figure it out."

"It's not just that. There are so many things I can't explain." Katie knew something wasn't right with Tessa. And it went beyond Rose and The Box and resenting Mark. "I get the feeling it has to do with the fire."

Dr. Capello frowned and checked her watch. "I wish I could help you, but I've got appointments in town. I'm already late. . . ."

"Great," Katie said, feeling butterflies in her stomach at what she was about to do. But she couldn't just stand around doing nothing. "Let's go," she said, and opened the passenger door. She set Dr. Capello's briefcase on the floor with her book bag.

"Um, Katie?" The psychiatrist peered over the hood. "What are you doing?"

"I'm going with you," she said, because it was the only way. "I have to find someone who was there the night Tessa's house burned. Someone like Virginia Cottingham," she said, remembering the name of the neighbor from the article in the *Barnard Gazette* that she'd read on Tessa's MacBook. "So if you'd drop me off at Mayfield Avenue, that'd be perfect."

"No," Dr. Capello told her.

"What? Oh, sorry." Katie cleared her throat. "Will you drop me off at Mayfield Avenue, *please,*" she said, then got into the car and pulled on the seat belt with a click.

Dr. Capello slid in behind the wheel but didn't close the door. The car made a soft dinging noise as she spoke. "Being polite isn't the problem. I can't take you into Barnard without clearance from your mom or the headmaster."

"Oh."

Katie speed-dialed her mom and prayed she'd pick up. "Hey, yeah, it's me," she said, relieved when she heard the worried voice at the other end. "I'm all right, I swear. I just need you to give Dr. Capello permission to take me into Barnard for a bit. I have something pretty important to do. It shouldn't take long."

She pushed her phone toward Dr. Capello and couldn't help but smile the littlest bit. "As long as I've got a responsible adult along, my mom's cool with it. And I'd say you're responsible enough." When the psychiatrist hesitated, Katie asked, "You want to speak to her privately? Or would you like to hear her say yes on speaker?"

Dr. Capello gave Katie a look before taking the phone and speaking briefly to her mother. When she was done she stabbed the key in the ignition. "Okay," she said, shaking her head a bit as if to say, *You'd better not make me regret this.*

When they got to Mayfield Avenue, Dr. Capello's Volvo crept up to the address where Tessa had once lived. Katie half expected to see the blackened shell of a house from the online photo. Instead, there was a quaint-looking Victorian sitting behind a white picket fence. Someone had rebuilt on the spot. Katie wondered who'd want to put up a house on soil where three people had tragically died.

"It's been ten years. Even when something horrible happens, life goes on," the psychiatrist said, clearly knowing where Katie's thoughts had gone.

The mailbox on the house next door had faded white letters that spelled out COTTINGHAM, which made things all too easy.

"This is it," Katie said, and the Volvo came to a stop.

Before Dr. Capello dropped Katie off, the shrink made her swear she'd call as soon as she was finished. She had to promise, too, that she wouldn't go anywhere else on her own. "If anything happened to you . . . ," Dr. Capello said, but Katie assured her, "It won't."

The Volvo idled at the curb as Katie walked to the front door and rang the bell. *What if no one's home?* she worried for a moment until she heard the lock turn.

A heavyset older woman answered. "Yes?" she said. Her white hair was close-cropped, her eyes thick-lidded. "Can I help you?"

"Are you Virginia Cottingham?"

"Oh, hon, if you're here to sell candy or cookies to raise money for your glee club or band, I can't do it. I've got diabetes, and I have to watch my weight." She patted her belly, which stretched her knit top so that the zigzag pattern looked like stripes.

"I'm not selling anything," Katie told her. "I'd like to ask you some questions about a girl who used to live next door. Tessa Lupinski."

The woman's baggy eyes narrowed. "The child who survived the fire?"

"Yes."

"Is she in trouble? It wouldn't surprise me if she was," the woman murmured. "Those kids were both odd ducks."

"She's not in trouble exactly, she's"—*talking crazy, trying to get my boyfriend locked up*, Katie wasn't sure what to say—"my roommate at Whitney Prep, and I'm very worried about her."

Mrs. Cottingham's face closed off for a minute, and Katie thought she was going to shut the door. But instead, she opened it wider. "If we're going to talk you might as well come in."

Katie turned and waved to the Volvo before it finally took off. "My ride," she explained. "She'll be back to pick me up."

"It's good to be careful these days," the woman said as she gestured for Katie to enter. She sat down on a floral-patterned sofa, taking care not to unsettle a black cat sprawled across the cushions. "It's a scary world we live in, isn't it?" she remarked, and absently began to stroke the sleeping feline. "You'd figure nothing much would happen in a town like this. First to have the house burn down next door and then to have that young waitress from the diner go missing."

Katie cleared her throat. "I read an article from the *Gazette* about the fire. In it, you said you wouldn't be surprised if Peter Lupinski was responsible."

The woman nodded, the skin beneath her neck wobbling. "There was always something off about him. He drove his mother to distraction. Tanya would be over here, red-faced, asking if I'd seen him. He used to steal from her. And then he'd disappear for days. It broke her heart." She stopped petting the cat. "They came from an orphanage in Russia, you know. Tanya said they were badly neglected and malnourished, Peter most of all because he'd been there longer. I read up on it some. Those poor babies get no affection, none. It makes them go numb." Her gaze drifted over to the window. "I once saw him race around on his bike, run it into a tree, and fall hard on the concrete. You would've thought he'd cry his lungs out. Only he didn't. Kid had blood all over and lost some teeth, but his expression didn't change a hair."

Katie sat very still, trying to imagine what it had been like for Tessa and Peter, first living in an orphanage and then trying to adjust to being a family. If you shut down your emotions for too long to protect yourself, it couldn't be easy to turn them on again. No wonder Tessa didn't want to talk about it.

"He had a speech impediment," Mrs. Cottingham went on, and waved a blue-veined hand. "I'm not sure of the technical name, but he was tongue-tied. He didn't talk much. And when he did, he was hard to understand. As far as I know, he didn't have any friends. Except"—her face bunched up like she had smelled something putrid—"when he brought that riffraff home. Kids who looked like they hadn't washed in weeks. Tanya would find them in her kitchen, eating her food, sometimes sleeping in her sheets. Horrifying." She sniffed. "But more than anything, she was afraid for the little girl. In the end, all they wanted was to save her."

"What about Tessa?" Katie asked. "Was she reckless like Peter?"

"Quite the opposite." The woman began stroking the cat again, eliciting a gentle purr. "She was a quiet mouse. I saw her with her mom in the garden sometimes. I used to wave at her and say hello, but I don't think she ever said boo to me."

That sounded like Tessa, Katie thought. Reserved to the point of being standoffish.

"She loved her brother, though, I'll tell you that." Mrs. Cottingham nodded. "If he was anywhere near, she clung to him like she was drowning and he was her life raft."

Tessa must have felt completely lost when her brother had died along with the only parents she'd ever known. Was that the reason she couldn't move past it? Or was there something more that Katie wasn't seeing yet? "You don't think Tessa set the fire, do you?" she finally asked, thinking of the rumors she'd heard since she'd come to Whitney Prep.

The woman hesitated for a few seconds before she shook

her head, setting her chin to wobbling again. "No," she said, "I truly don't. I always believed it was him. Tessa was only seven when it happened. He was twelve, practically a teenager. There was still hope for her. But him . . ."

"Hopeless?"

"Yes."

"Did anyone ever find out who rescued Tessa that night?"

"Not as far as I know," the woman said, puffing air through her lips. "I recall the firemen saying it was a miracle she'd survived without burns, that whoever got her out must've suffered for it. But no one ever came forward."

Tessa had told Katie that "a ghost" had saved her. It sounded close enough to the truth. Who else could have done something so heroic and then disappeared like a wisp of smoke?

"Tanya and John just tried to do what was right, and that boy destroyed them all. He couldn't be saved. He had no heart," Mrs. Cottingham said, and put a finger to her lips as though to steady herself.

Katie could see that the woman had more she wanted to say, so she let her talk.

"About a week before the fire, Mr. Whiskers went missing."

"Mr. Whiskers?"

"My dear cat." Her red-rimmed eyes filled with tears. "He was more like my child. I'd had him for fifteen years. Got him when my husband passed. I should never have let him outside, but he liked to wander over to Tanya's garden next door, and I never thought a thing about it."

"What happened? Did he die?" Katie asked, and the woman's face quickly went from sad to angry.

"Did he die?" she repeated so fiercely she left spittle on her chin. "That evil boy killed him! I couldn't prove it, but I know it's true." She tugged roughly on the hem of her zigzag shirt. "The day before the fire, I found a cardboard box tied with garden twine left on my porch." She made noises like tiny sobs and then cleared her throat. "When I opened it up, Mr. Whiskers was inside, stiff as a board." Her rheumy eyes looked up. Her mouth trembled. "I couldn't prove it but I know that boy poisoned him. And if he could murder Mr. Whiskers in cold blood, he was capable of anything."

CHAPTER TWENTY-ONE

KATIE

Katie left Virginia Cottingham's house feeling strangely wired, like she'd had too many caffeine shots. Her head swirled with what she'd learned about Tessa and Peter Lupinski, things she'd never known, stuff Tessa would never have told her in a million years. But instead of getting all the answers she wanted, she ended up with more questions.

Like, who had saved Tessa from the fire? How far could someone with burns go without getting help? Had Peter killed Mrs. Cottingham's cat and set it on her porch in a box tied with twine? It was so eerily similar to the box with the hand that Katie couldn't shake the sense that the two were connected.

There was something else that kept nagging at the back of Katie's brain about Tessa and The Box, but she couldn't put her finger on it.

The worst part of all was that Katie found herself wondering if her best friend might be involved with what had happened to Rose. Was that the reason Tessa was so determined to place the blame on Mark? Maybe it had nothing to do with being jealous and was all about saving herself.

Oh, God, what's going on?

The more she dug, the more complicated everything got.

She stood on Mrs. Cottingham's porch for a moment before calling Dr. Capello. There was one more place she needed to go before she went back to school. It wouldn't take long. She hoped the school psychiatrist was busy with a session and wouldn't try to stop her.

"Hey, Dr. C, it's Katie," she started to say when a voice answered, "Hello, this is Dr. Lisa Capello," but it was only voice mail.

Katie took a deep breath and rambled on after the beep, "Yeah, I know you told me to stay put, but I need to visit the Lupinskis' graves, and I'm only three blocks from the cemetery. Maybe you could pick me up there. I swear, I'll be careful."

She quickly hung up, her heart racing, expecting her phone to ring and Dr. Capello to bawl her out and tell her not to go anywhere. But when she didn't hear anything within a few minutes, Katie took it as a sign and started walking.

It was a bright and mild April afternoon, and she didn't feel the least bit nervous as she took the sidewalk toward the town center. An orange school bus rumbled by on the road, and she passed several dog walkers and a mother pushing her baby in a stroller.

When Katie got to the cemetery, she stopped outside the gates.

Even though the sun perched high in an impeccably blue sky, there was something ominous about the wrought-iron gates with the arched entry flanked by two solemn Victorian angels carved from stone and discolored by time and pollution; their hands were clasped in prayer, weathered faces tipped toward the clouds as though desperately seeking permission to depart their sooty pedestals and return to the sanctity of heaven.

It was very Gothic, Katie thought, kind of *Twilight* meets *Jane Eyre,* and creepy enough to make her shudder. After such a gloomy greeting, she appreciated the cheerful pots of marigolds inside the gates and yellow daffodils that speckled the lawn between burial plots.

She had to stop and ask the groundskeeper where the Lupinskis were buried, and he pointed her toward the pond, where dappled sunlight danced.

"Look for an elm tree with a concrete bench beneath it," he told her, and Katie thanked him.

She could hear the occasional whoosh of cars beyond the fence and the squawk of ducks and geese. No one else was about, so the grounds seemed ungodly quiet save for the scrape of her shoes on the gravel road and the twitter of birds.

Katie paused as she came to a curve in the path, the duck pond just yards away.

Headstones and monuments rose from the grass, serenaded by chirping birds and shaded by trees, branches swaying in the breeze. She wended her way through family plots, squinting at unfamiliar names and moving on. She passed a dozen before she saw the one engraved JOHN HENRY LUPINSKI, BELOVED HUSBAND AND FATHER.

Beside it was the marker for Tanya Lupinski. The tombstone for Peter Mikhail Lupinski sat at least a dozen feet away. Maybe the space between was reserved for Tessa? Or maybe they just hadn't wanted Peter so near even after they were gone.

Her phone rang, cutting through the quiet of the graveyard, and Katie felt relieved when she saw the number was Bea Lively's.

"You found something?" she said, staring at the duck pond as she waited for Bea's answer.

"That's what's weird," Bea replied in a hushed voice. "I didn't find anything. Nothing at all. Steve's transcript for this past semester at Whitney and all his transferred records have no remarks regarding discipline."

"None?"

"None. So either he's a Boy Scout with a bad rap, or someone's done a great job of scrubbing his records."

"Nothing?" Katie croaked, unable to believe it.

"Nada, zip, zilch." Bea sighed loudly. "I even poked into my own file and yours to make sure it wasn't a glitch in the system. We both had disciplinary notes about that sit-in at the cafeteria last November, so it's not like Big Brother wiped out everything."

"Too bad."

"Yeah, no kidding. I glanced at Tessa's transcript, too, just to be sure," Bea went on in the same hushed tone. "Even she had a blot on her record from way back when she first started at Whitney."

"Really?" Katie couldn't imagine what Tessa had done. Ever since she'd known her, Tessa had been all about "we scholly kids have to go by the book."

"Apparently she stole some stuff."

"From another student?"

"No, from the dorm kitchen," Bea told her. "She took food. Tins of fruit and bags of bread. They found a hoard of it in the basement machine room. Maybe she had the opposite of anorexia, whatever that is."

"Yeah, maybe." Katie wondered if hoarding food was a hangover from Tessa's days at the orphanage. The neighbor had said that Tessa and Peter had been malnourished.

"Anyway, I'm sorry I couldn't help you nail that prick Steve, but his record's a big, fat blank."

"Thanks, Bea," Katie said, and hung up.

She sank down on the grass, biting her cheek and screwing up her nerve before she pulled up the Whitney website on her phone, entered her password, and found what she needed in the school directory. Then she dialed Joelle Needham's number.

"It's Katie," she said the second Joelle answered. "I wanted you to know I got into Steve's records, but his transcripts don't show he was ever disciplined for anything. There's no proof that he ever hurt anyone. If you don't step up and talk—"

Joelle hung up on her.

Katie sighed and put her phone away. She'd tried, right? She'd done her best, but she didn't know where else to look. She wasn't a cop or a forensics expert. There wasn't much else she could do.

For a long time, she just stared at Peter Lupinski's gravestone, her thoughts so confused it made her head hurt.

I think it was a ghost . . . I wish he'd left me there . . . whoever got her out must've suffered for it . . .

What if—Katie's exhausted brain began to wonder—what if Tessa's brother had saved her from the fire, the same way he'd protected her in the orphanage? Was it possible he'd gotten Tessa out safely and then gone back into the house?

He brought riffraff home . . . kids who looked like they hadn't washed in weeks . . . Tanya would find them in her kitchen, eating her food, sometimes sleeping in her sheets.

Or maybe he hadn't gone back in at all. Could the charred bones buried in Peter's grave belong to someone else? Was there any way—any chance—that Tessa's brother could still be alive?

A chill crept up her spine despite the warm afternoon.

A twig snapped nearby, and Katie looked up as a shadow fell upon her, blotting out the sun. Before she could make out a face, she held her breath, her heart beating a million miles a minute, thinking it was Peter Lupinski, risen from the dead.

CHAPTER TWENTY-TWO

MARK

Run, Mark's brain had told him. *Just run.*

After the cops had pulled the strange phone from his locker and were yakking on their walkie-talkies, Mark got on his cell, dialing a number he'd looked up but hadn't screwed up the nerve to call. His head down, he'd hurried past his teammates despite Steve Getty calling out, "Hey, Summers, where d'you think you're goin'?"

Dr. Capello's secretary had answered and told Mark she wasn't there, that she was at her office in town. So he'd left a voice mail, begging for help. "If you can do anything that'll make me remember that night, you have to do it," he'd pleaded. "No matter what I find out."

Then he'd grabbed his bike and hauled ass across campus, his adrenaline sky-high. He'd veered off the pavement, cutting to a dirt path that led through the woods. Wild vines and branches had batted at him as he rode, pushing hard with his thighs. By the time he'd bypassed the guardhouse and made it onto the rural road into Barnard, he was sweating buckets. His face dripped; his shirt stuck to his back. All the way into town, he'd thought about Katie and what she'd said to him after they'd found Rose.

You have *to remember! I've seen a dozen Lifetime movies where people get hypnotized and recover lost memories. Maybe you should try that. You have to do* something.

His phone had vibrated in his back pocket during the twenty minutes it took him to reach Barnard. When Mark finally pulled into the alley beside the hospital, it was just in time to catch a call from Dr. Capello. Before he could say more than "Hello," she started in about guided meditation to recover memories, telling him it wasn't reliable—that most shrinks thought of it as quackery—and the headmaster surely wouldn't approve. But Mark was eighteen, he didn't need his father's consent. "Please," he said, a catch in his throat, "it's the only way. I'm already in Barnard. I biked here—"

"Where are you?"

"By the hospital."

She got quiet for a minute, and he sensed she was about to blow him off. Instead, she murmured, "Okay," then added something weird: "Go across the street to the cemetery and wait. Katie's there, and I'm on my way to get her."

Katie was at the cemetery? *His* Katie?

Mark set his bike in the hospital rack and headed toward the cemetery's gates. He wandered around and was walking toward the duck pond when he spotted her. As he approached, she looked up, her eyes wide as quarters, like she'd just seen a ghost.

She scrambled to her feet.

"What are you doing here?" she asked, taking a step away.

Was she scared of him? He looked around, thinking maybe that was it because they were pretty much alone. Then he saw the markers on the plot where they were standing and knew it was more than that. She was spooked. "You came to see Tessa's family's graves?"

"I came to get answers," she said.

"Did you find them?"

She shrugged. "I'm still figuring things out." She picked up her bag and started walking toward the entrance.

"I'm here for answers, too," he told her, and followed. "Someone's playing me, but I don't know who. The cops found a disposable phone in my locker, but it's not mine. I don't know how it even got there—"

"A disposable phone?" Katie stopped and gave him a look. "Like in Tessa's story?"

Mark squinted. "What story?"

"She's saying you drunk-dialed her the night of the party and told her you'd killed Rose. That you were using Rose's phone when you asked her to help you cover it up. It had an anonymous number, like a prepaid." Her brown eyes watched him as he tried to digest what she was saying, but it made no sense at all. "You seriously didn't know?"

"It's been a pretty wild day," Mark said, touching the

168

bruise on his brow, feeling like he'd taken another stick to the head. "I thought Steve was behind this but Tessa's involved?"

"I'm not sure what's going on," Katie murmured, biting her lip. "I think Tessa's trying to protect someone. It's crazy, but I was wondering if—never mind."

"You were wondering if it was Steve?"

"No, not Steve. It can't be. Tessa despises him." Katie shook her head. "I'm not sure who it is or what Tessa's up to, but I'm worried."

"Maybe that won't matter once I can remember." Mark swallowed a hard lump in his throat. "Dr. Capello's agreed to put me under."

"You're getting hypnotized?" Katie looked genuinely shocked.

"I have to find out what I've forgotten." He ran a hand through his sweat-damp hair. "It's worth a shot, right? 'Cause if I can't put the pieces together, it's game over."

Maybe it was just a trick of the light, but Mark thought he saw Katie's eyes brighten. "I hope it works," she said.

"Will you stay with me while I do it?" Mark asked as a Volvo pulled up in the street outside the gates. They walked toward it.

"Sure," she said quietly. "If you want me there, I'll stay."

The blinds had been pulled, shutting out the pink of dusk. Dr. Capello sat in an armchair near the recliner where Mark lay. Katie was there but he couldn't see her. She was some-where behind him, quiet as a mouse.

"Focus on breathing deeply and evenly," the psychiatrist instructed in a firm but gentle tone, and Mark tried hard to do as she asked. "Feel your muscles turn to jelly, inch by inch," she said. "Begin with the tips of your toes and your feet, now your ankles and calves, your knees . . ."

On and on she went, working her way to the top of his head.

Mark sensed his pulse easing and his breaths coming deeper and farther apart. He envisioned every muscle in his body turning limp, bit by bit, until his chin drooped onto his chest.

"Picture a place that you love where you're at ease and without worries. Imagine yourself there right this minute."

Mark saw himself looking down at bare feet stepping into dew-damp grass. Ahead of him was the lake house where his dad used to take him fishing. The whitewashed cottage was surrounded by trees so thick he felt swallowed by green.

"Are you there?" a voice asked softly. "If you are, lift your right index finger."

Mark lifted his finger.

He breathed in cedar from the plank walls and the stale scent of smoke from the fireplace. He heard water lapping at the sand and the lonely cry of a whip-poor-will. If he could have stayed there forever, he would.

"Turn around slowly, and you'll see a red door," the voice urged. "Is it there?"

His finger twitched.

"Turn the knob and pass through. When you do, you'll step into the headmaster's house. It's Saturday night two weekends ago, and your father's away. You're having a party with your friends. Describe who's there and what you see."

Mark went through the red door and emerged in the basement rec room, the walls blurred with color from the lava lamps. Music blared, the bass thumping, and he heard voices and laughter.

Charlie's sitting by himself, drinking beer from a red Solo cup. He's watching from across the room. He doesn't like that townies are there. Getty brought them when he went into Barnard to get a keg from the dude at the liquor store who doesn't care that anyone's underage so long as you pay double in cash.

When I tell Steve the girls have to go, he just hands me a cup from the keg. "Get the stick out of your ass and relax. Drink up." He grins and walks away.

The blonde's laughing a little too loudly, banging into furniture because she can't walk straight. I think both townies were already drunk or high before they got here, and I'm glad I locked the liquor cabinet. The blonde turns up the music and starts dancing around, doing a sad striptease till she's tripping over the guys in her underwear.

The other girl, the brunette, looks a little like Katie. She's got dark eyes and the same long, dark hair. But there's something cheap about her: too much makeup, too many earrings, too-tight clothes. Getty doesn't seem to mind. They're leaning in and whispering like they've got a secret. Then the dark-haired one heads for the stairs.

I ask where she's going but she doesn't hear. I don't want her on the first floor. What if she breaks something? Or steals stuff?

"Hey!" I start after her, but Steve stops me dead. He pats me on the back and says, "Dude, loosen up. We're celebrating, aren't we? It's not like you're gonna drink and drive, right? You're home already."

I try to chill and sip my beer.

Charlie's watching with this weird expression. My head's so foggy, like I'm tired and can't think straight. Charlie gets up and comes toward me, but I'm going upstairs. I wonder where the brunette went, and I need some air.

The blonde staggers forward, but I get out of her way. I grab the banister and drag myself up, bumping into the console in the hallway. Charlie's behind me, asking if I'm okay. I can hardly stand up straight. I drop my beer and stumble toward the back door. I want to get out of there, get outside where I can breathe. Something's wrong with me, and I don't know what it is.

But I don't make it.

I fall to my knees. I can't stand anymore. Something bad's going on. Something's seriously messed up. I puke but nothing comes out. I smell this putrid perfume and a girl's bending over me, her dark hair hanging down. I think it's Katie—I want it to be Katie—but it's not.

Charlie's disappeared.

The girl puts her arm around my waist, and I can't stand without her holding me up. I hear the music from the basement, but it sounds so far away. I'm so messed up that I don't realize where she's taking me until she pushes me onto a bed, and I see the crucifix on the wall, over the dresser.

I feel her unbuttoning my shirt, tugging it off. I can hardly breathe with her weight on top of me. I want to push her away, but I can't lift my arms. I can't do anything but lie there like I'm dead. I try to open my eyes but they're too heavy.

Someone whispers, "Put your hand on his chest, yeah, like that. Lean over and kiss him. Yeah, yeah. Do that."

Steve?

The voice says, "Come here," and her weight lifts from my chest. I don't know if they're still in the room or if they've left.

I black out for a while and when I come to I hear someone saying, "Get up, dammit! Get up!" And then Charlie's voice, sounding scared. "She's not breathing, dude. She's not breathing."

"Let me handle this."

"Is she dead—"

"I'll take care of it."

"We should call someone. . . ."

"No. You hear me? No. Now get out of here."

Mark started thrashing, throwing his head back and forth. Was Rose in the room with him, dead? Why couldn't he see? He needed to open his eyes and see.

"Take it easy." The soft voice became firm. "You need to come out of this slowly, do you hear me? Do you see a red door? Walk toward it and turn the knob—"

But Mark didn't have time for the door. He fought his way out. He was done. *Through.* He wasn't the one who saw what happened to Rose. He couldn't remember because he didn't know.

Wake up, wake up, wake up.

With a groan, he emerged, peering around the room, disoriented. Katie came around the chair, and he felt tears in his eyes as he looked at her.

"Charlie knows," he said, choking up. "He barefaced lied to me. He was right there in the room. Did Steve kill that girl?" He rubbed a hand across his jaw. "Or did I?"

But Katie couldn't answer. How could she know if he didn't?

"Oh, shit, they'll arrest me, won't they? If Charlie knows I wasn't involved but keeps it to himself, I'm going to jail. I've got nothing, no proof that it wasn't me, and the police keep stacking up the circumstantial evidence."

"Mark, you need to calm down," Dr. Capello said, putting a hand on his arm.

He shook her off.

The phone on the desk started ringing.

Mark cringed at the noise.

"I'm sorry, but I should get it," she said. "It's the back line, for emergencies. . . ."

"Go ahead, we're done." Mark shakily pulled himself upright, leaning forearms on his knees. "It doesn't matter anymore."

Katie didn't come over. She didn't put her arms around him and tell him everything would be okay. She wrapped her arms around herself, her face a mix of confusion and misery.

"Yes, I'll be right there." Dr. Capello hung up the phone and grabbed her keys. "We have to get back to Whitney now. It's Charlie Fraser."

Mark gritted his teeth. "What about him?"

"He's in the school clinic, getting his stomach pumped," she replied matter-of-factly, and gestured toward the door. "His roommate found him on the floor, barely breathing."

CHAPTER TWENTY-THREE

TESSA

Tessa paced like a caged cat.

She had to get out of Amelia House.

She'd been deposited there with a warning to stay put after the campus police had made her repeat her story again and again, once with the headmaster sitting across the table, his face a scary shade of purple. They'd confiscated her cell phone, so she couldn't call out unless she used the house line, and you never knew if someone else might be listening in. She was a prisoner, trapped in her own dormitory. She'd heard the security chief tell Mrs. Gabbert to keep an eye on her, and campus cops were watching the back and front doors. It was as though she'd committed a crime instead of finally telling the truth.

And it *was* the truth in many ways, or as close as she could get without making a huge sacrifice she wasn't willing to make.

It wasn't like Tessa had imagined the headmaster would pat her on the back after she'd accused his son of murder. But she hadn't figured she'd be treated like *she* was the guilty one. She didn't think they'd keep her trapped inside without a phone or an easy way out.

And where was Katie during all this? Hardly being a supportive friend. Tessa hadn't seen her since the blowup at the school shrink's office. She probably just needed time to cool off, time to think. When the cops found the dead girl's phone, they'd believe Tessa, at least about getting a call from Rose's number. Then Katie would have no choice but to believe her, too.

The cops would arrest Mark, wouldn't they? Tessa had seen more black-and-whites on campus today. Maybe they'd already done it. Unless . . . unless . . .

A pang of worry struck her chest.

What if Mark was on the run, hiding in the tunnels? She knew he went there a lot, and not only because Katie had told her. She'd seen him, had followed him to the greenhouse more than once.

If the police were out looking, if they got Katie to mention the tunnels, that could mean big, big trouble. Tessa had to slip out of Amelia House. She couldn't risk the cops going underground and stumbling upon something they shouldn't.

Someone they shouldn't.

She wasn't worried about herself. It had never been about her. Everything Tessa had ever done—every lie she'd ever told—was to protect the two people she loved the most.

It was the least she could do. They'd both saved her in more ways than one.

She grabbed her key chain with the penlight and stuck it in her blazer pocket. Then she went into the closet and stuffed a bunch of clothes into her laundry bag, even though she'd signed up to do wash two days before so most everything was clean. If anyone asked where she was going, at least she'd have a good explanation.

She ducked down the back stairwell, her shoes clanking on the metal stairs as she took them two by two. Her heart was thumping madly in her chest by the time she reached the basement. She worried that some of the girls would be watching TV, and they were.

So she did something she'd done once before: she opened the electrical box hanging on the wall above one of the washing machines, and she tripped the switch for the basement. One little *click* and the place went dark.

"What's going on? I can't see."

"What if it's the killer . . ."

Tessa heard shrieks as the girls who'd been staring at the wide-screen fumbled their way out of the room and toward the stairs. They'd go crying to Mrs. Gabbert, which was all the time Tessa needed.

She left her laundry bag on the floor and hurried through the dark. Her nerves tingling, she pushed open the door to the machine room. She squeezed the penlight and used its tiny glow to guide her toward the loosened grate. Though she was small, she wasn't weak, and it was easy enough to move the metal cover aside, allowing her to slip into the old steam tunnels.

She made her way through the passages easily. She'd known about the tunnels even before she'd turned eleven and enrolled at Whitney Prep on scholarship. Though their dad had brought Peter to campus more often than her, Tessa had tagged along on occasion. Peter had discovered the tunnels first. He loved the quiet, dark passages. He'd learned his way around them like a rat through a maze. It wasn't long before he'd started hiding down there, infuriating their father, who'd been unable to find him. He'd left Peter there a few times, once overnight. Tessa had known exactly where he was when Peter hadn't come home. When her brother resurfaced and was punished, he didn't even seem to mind. "When ahm in tunnel no one bug meh. No one yell or call meh names," he'd told her, talking in the funny way that got him teased at school. But Tessa had no problem understanding. She never had.

But she hadn't been as fond of the tunnels. She'd had to get used to the dark and that didn't happen until she was older. Once her parents were dead, once she was out of the foster home and living at Whitney, she began spending more time underground, and she learned to appreciate the things Peter loved most about it. In some ways, it felt easier being down there than anywhere else. There was no one to gossip about her. No one to remark that she wasn't smart enough or pretty enough. There was just the dark and the chilly air and the noise of footsteps scraping the stone.

As she moved through the tunnels now, they felt so

familiar, her home. She still used the penlight but she knew where to go. It wasn't long before she felt a presence in the passageway behind her.

She knew who it was without him saying a word. He smelled like the earth, cool and damp. Sometimes he smelled like greenhouse roses.

Tessa wanted to cry with relief. She'd been afraid she might not find him. He wasn't always where he should be. He'd begun going up more at night, doing things he shouldn't. That was how he'd gotten into trouble, why he'd called Tessa that night with the dead girl's phone, begging for help.

He touched her arm. "You have to be careful," Tessa said. "*Very* careful. More than you've ever been."

She heard a grunt in response as he came up close beside her.

"They can't find you. They can't know what you did."

He slipped the penlight from her fingers and turned it off. Then he reached for her hand and held it firmly. His scarred flesh felt rough and reassuring as he drew her along. By now, he had eyes like a mole's. He didn't need light as he moved through the pitch-black.

His breath came noisily. It had ever since the fire. He'd breathed in so much smoke his lungs were probably as scarred as his skin. No matter how he looked, how he sounded, he didn't scare Tessa. He never had. Why should he when he was the reason she'd lived? If not for him, she wouldn't be here. She'd be buried in the Barnard cemetery along with her adoptive parents and a boy whose name she'd never even known.

CHAPTER TWENTY-FOUR

MARK

At first when Mark saw Charlie, he thought his friend was dead.

He lay so still beneath the white sheet. His skin was beyond pale, like all the blood had been drained from him. He had tubes in his nose for oxygen and an IV taped to his wrist that dripped fluids into his veins.

According to the school's doctor, Charlie had taken a shit-ton of Ambien. They didn't think he'd make it at first. Thank God his roommate found him soon after and called the clinic. They'd brought him in and pumped his stomach. He'd flatlined at one point, and they had to paddle his chest, but his heart had started beating again.

"He's not going anywhere," the doctor said, patting Mark on the back, "though he'll feel like hell when he wakes up."

Mark didn't even know his dad was at the clinic until he

heard his voice. "They're moving him to the hospital in Barnard when he's a little more stable. Dr. Capello's sticking around to help him deal with things when he wakes up. The police will want to talk to him, too, but not tonight."

"The police?" Mark pulled his gaze away from Charlie's face. "Because he tried to kill himself?"

"He left you a note," his father said, reaching into his pocket and pulling out a piece of folded paper. "This is a copy, sorry. The police wanted the original. He's been keeping secrets, Mark. About you and Steve Getty and that poor girl Rose. He makes it clear you're not to blame."

"You read it?" Mark took the page from his dad, feeling sad and angry at once.

"It was with him when he was found. We needed to know if it explained why. I just wish he'd come forward sooner," his father said.

Then he left Mark alone to read the letter.

I'm sorry, Summers, because I wasn't honest with you. When you asked if I knew anything about that night, I should have told you the truth. But you were right. I was scared, too scared to talk. That asshole Getty was holding something over my head. He had pictures, video, of me with another guy. I know, I should have told you. You wouldn't have cared, right? But not everyone's that cool with having a gay teammate. Getty knew I was afraid that word would spread and Minnesota would pull my scholly. "What

college would recruit a fag? This is hockey, not ballet,"
he said, and he was right. Fuck it, but he was right.
So I kept quiet. I should have told you that you didn't
have anything to do with Rose dying. You were out cold
the whole time. Steve wouldn't tell me what he slipped
you, but he gave you something. He took pictures of you
with the girl. That's how he controls people. If he can't
get them to look bad on their own, he does it for them.
Rose was already high on X and Getty gave her more.
He said she started choking on her own puke and OD'd
right there on the floor. He put your chain around her
neck so if they blamed anyone, they'd blame you. He
wanted to leave her there so they'd find her with you.
But I couldn't do it.

After the other guys left, when Getty took the blonde
home, I carried her down to the basement. I put her
in that back room with the old furnace. I meant to tell
you what happened in the morning when you woke
up. But she was gone, dude. I swear, she was gone. I
thought Steve had come back. I thought he took her.
But he was pissed at me for moving her. I screwed up
his plan.

He swore he didn't cut off her hand. He said he
didn't know where she was, and I believe him. He
looked afraid, not knowing where she'd gone to. I was
pretty freaked out, too.

But then she was found and the cops were all over
you. I'm sorry, man, I should've been brave. I should

*have told Steve to go to hell. But I didn't, and I've
hated myself ever since. I hope you forgive me someday.
I let you down, bro. I let myself down, too.*

Charlie

Mark's hands shook as he finished. He glanced at Charlie's face, at the crooked nose that had been broken and never set, and he thought of how they'd grown up together at Whitney. He thought of all the times they'd studied for exams, all the hockey they'd watched and the games they'd played. And still Charlie hadn't come to him before he tried to take his own life. It made no sense.

He leaned over his friend and gazed at his eyes closed in sleep, wishing he'd known. Wishing Charlie had talked to him. He couldn't imagine a secret worth anybody's life.

"Charlie," he whispered. "They'll get him, man. They'll put him away. He won't be a threat anymore, not to you, not to me, not to anyone."

Charlie's eyelids fluttered.

Mark bent closer. "You awake? You need the doctor?"

"Steve," Charlie breathed.

Mark nodded down at him. "Yeah, Steve's going down, dude. You don't need to worry about him."

"No," Charlie exhaled, and wet his lips. "He's mad . . . at Katie. . . ."

"Steve's mad at Katie? Why?"

"Joelle," Charlie got out in a whisper, then his eyes slipped closed again.

Mark squeezed his shoulder. "It'll be okay," he said. "I promise."

"Sweet." Charlie went back to sleep.

The fluid dripped into the IV. Oxygen gently hissed. Charlie's chest rose and fell. He was clearly out of it.

Mark stood up slowly, his heart thudding. He had the letter in his hand, and he had to tell Katie. She'd come into the clinic with him and the psychiatrist but had hung back in the waiting room. He didn't see her there now. Instead, Joelle was thumbing through an old magazine. When she saw him, she stood up.

"Is Charlie okay?" she asked.

Mark nodded. "He will be. He saw what happened, Jo." He raised the hand that held the letter. "He said the girl OD'd when she was with Steve. It wasn't me."

"I'm glad." Joelle's usually perfectly made-up face had smudges beneath the eyes and streaks down her cheeks where she'd wiped away tears. "Steve's about to get hit with a big damn stick," she said, and let out a sad laugh. "I already told him I'm not staying quiet any longer . . . about what he did to me. It wasn't what you thought," she said, shaking her head, and the tears starting falling. "I'm ready to talk."

"I'm sorry, Jo. I really am." Mark didn't know what else to say. He felt awful that he hadn't listened to her.

"I told Steve that Katie was right. If someone didn't speak up and make him stop, he'd do it again. There'd be another me, another Rose."

"You told Steve Katie said that?"

Joelle nodded. "Yeah. That girl's got balls, you know. She's not the mousy mouse I thought."

"Where is she?" Mark asked, looking around but not seeing Katie anywhere.

"She was heading out just when I got here," Jo told him. "She nearly ran into me. She got a text from Tessa, and she was all worked up about it. She said it was weird, that it wasn't Tessa's number, but I told her about Tessa pissing off the headmaster and being put on lockdown at the dorm. I heard they took her phone."

Mark remembered Katie mentioning Tessa's "confession" about him calling her the night Rose died and saying that he did it. Yeah, he was sure that would have pissed off his dad enough to have Mrs. Gabbert sit on Tessa for a while. But now his father knew the truth. He couldn't wait to show Katie Charlie's note. Then she'd realize that her buddy Tessa had been lying through her teeth.

He speed-dialed Katie's number. "C'mon, pick up," he said, as it rang and rang before finally going to voice mail. "Where are you?"

Then he texted her, asking the same question.

But she didn't answer.

Mark felt his gut twist, and he suddenly thought of something Katie had said when he'd found her staring at Peter Lupinski's grave.

I think Tessa's trying to protect someone. It's crazy, but I was wondering if— Never mind . . . I'm not sure who it is or what Tessa's up to, but I'm worried.

Who was Tessa protecting? Could it be Steve? Was that why Katie had mentioned that what she was thinking was crazy?

Charlie had whispered something about Steve being mad at Katie. Was it because she'd been stirring things up?

He walked away from Joelle, heading toward the exit. As soon as the sliding glass doors parted before him, he took off running toward Amelia House.

Dusk had descended, and streetlights dotted the dark overhead as he sprinted. The path across campus was almost empty. Mark was winded by the time he reached Amelia House, but he didn't slow down to catch his breath. He didn't even stop when he saw the security guard getting out of the campus police car across the street. Mark's feet kept moving till he reached the door.

"Katie!" He started banging the door with his fists. "Katie!"

"Hold on there," the guard called out, one hand on his stun gun and the other tapping his shoulder walkie-talkie.

But Mark kept banging until the housemother opened the door.

"For heaven's sake, what's going on?" The older woman frowned at him.

"I need to see Katie," Mark said, breathing hard. "It's important. Can you ask her to come down, please?"

Mrs. Gabbert glanced past him at the security guard. "She's not here. I haven't seen her all day, not since she left for class this morning."

A bunch of girls had begun to gather behind the housemother inside the foyer. Mark glanced at their anxious faces.

"Is Tessa around?" he asked, sure she'd know where Katie was. He figured Katie would be with her.

"Of course. She's been here since the security chief dropped her off hours ago." The housemother disappeared for a moment, and Mark shifted impatiently from foot to foot. When she came back, her frown had deepened. "Tessa's not in her room, and the girls don't know where she is." Mrs. Gabbert's eyes teared up. "The lights in the basement went out just a moment ago. The breaker was tripped. You don't think Tessa did that?"

What Mark thought was that Katie was in trouble. And if Steve was involved, he had a damned good idea where they'd gone.

CHAPTER TWENTY-FIVE

KATIE

Meet me @ the rink ASAP, the text said, **life or death!!! Tessa**

Kind of dramatic, Katie thought as she headed out of the clinic, even for Tessa. Maybe Katie should have said no because she was exhausted and starving. She'd hardly slept the past two weeks, had hardly eaten all day. She felt weak and on edge and confused. But after seeing the Lupinskis' graves and getting a better grasp of what Tessa's life had been like before Whitney Prep, she couldn't turn her down. Tessa was her friend. Whatever the reason behind her crazy behavior, Katie owed her a chance to explain.

The phone number had been blocked. Tessa had probably borrowed someone's phone at the dorm. Joelle had mentioned Tessa being stuck at Amelia House without her cell. It was strange that she'd picked the ice rink, which was Mark's turf, not Tessa's. Was it because she was taking the tunnels there and the ice rink was the closest school building? The whole rec complex would be empty. All events on campus had been canceled after Rose's body had been found. So long as Katie didn't have to stumble through tunnels to get there, she didn't care. She just wanted this long day to be over and done with.

The air outside was crisp, the sky turning dark. An angry breeze rustled the branches of the trees above as she hurried up the sidewalk. Few students were out, and those who were walked in pairs. In an hour, the campus would be deserted. No one wanted to be wandering around by themselves after curfew until whoever killed Rose was caught.

The rink was part of a monstrous building that looked like the shadow of a dinosaur, hulking in the dark. Katie saw a campus police car slowly making its way past the building, shining its headlights on the facade before it rolled on.

Katie avoided the front doors, knowing they'd be locked. Tessa wouldn't need a key to get in—she'd be crawling through a grate. Katie went to the rear door that led to the lockers. When she'd come to the rink with Mark after-hours before, that was how they'd gotten in. Mark had told her it was rarely locked during hockey season since the guys came and went so much. It'd be easy enough to go through the locker room and into the rink, where Tessa was supposed to be waiting.

The light above the door weakly cast its beam on Katie as she approached and reached for the bar, pushing her way inside.

She stood in the dark, waiting as the door clanked shut behind her, listening for voices or noises that meant someone else was there. But she heard nothing.

With no one around, it couldn't hurt to flip the light switch, she figured. But when she clicked the switch back and forth, nothing came on. Maybe the bulbs were burned out.

As Katie's eyes adjusted, she caught the glistening of glass and brass in the dimly lit trophy case that lined the rear hallway. She started walking past it, glancing at all the ribbons and medals displayed alongside gleaming cups topped by figurines engaged in various sports. She paused in front of a sizable trophy topped by a pair of crossed hockey sticks. If she squinted, she could read Mark's name on the plaque at the base. MVP, PREP SCHOOL HOCKEY REGIONALS, it said. Katie knew how badly Mark wanted to put a state championship MVP trophy right beside it.

She wondered if Mark would even get to play now. Poor Charlie was clearly out of commission. Would Whitney go ahead if their star forward was arrested and their number one goalie in a hospital bed? Or would they forfeit with the game just two nights away?

She heard footsteps behind her and caught motion in the mirror at the back of the case. "Tessa?" she said, and turned.

"Sorry to disappoint you, but the Ice Princess isn't coming."

It was Steve Getty, and he stood between her and the door.

"I heard you've been sniffing around my shit," he said, and

took a step forward. "So I figured it was time we had a little chat."

"I have no clue what you mean," Katie said, stiffening.

"Joelle sent me a text. She's got this bright idea about going to the police. She said you convinced her to report me." He shook his head and made a *tsk-tsk* sound. "And you had someone poke into my records, didn't you? My dad's got a guy who monitors that stuff. Hacking Whitney's system is a piece of cake for a tech geek. Really stupid move," he said. "Someone should teach you to mind your own business."

"I'm not afraid of you," Katie said, even though it was a lie. He was twice her size, and for all she knew he'd murdered Rose Tatum. But what could he do that wouldn't come back to haunt him? He was a coward who pushed people around, who forced himself on girls, and who had very likely drugged a teammate. Would he shove her in a locker until someone found her in the morning? He couldn't do anything more without risking jail for real.

At least, that was what she told herself.

"I'm glad Joelle's coming forward," Katie said, the tiniest croak in her voice. "If you hurt her, you deserve whatever you get."

"I didn't do anything to Joelle that Joelle didn't want." Steve smiled, but there was malice in his eyes.

"And if you killed Rose," Katie went on, "I hope you rot for that, too."

"News flash, sweetheart," Steve said, and he wasn't smiling

anymore. His face went hard, and she saw his hands clench. "Your boyfriend's the one who killed the girl. Ask anyone."

"I don't have to," Katie replied, holding tight to her bag as Steve took a step nearer. "Mark doesn't drug girls and rough them up. That's your thing. What I don't get is why you sent me her hand. Was it to scare me? Were you trying to be funny after what happened at the morgue?"

"Christ!" Steve's face knotted with anger. "I didn't cut off that bitch's hand!"

"Then who did?" Katie's heart beat so fast she feared it would burst right out of her chest.

"I've gotta give props where props are due," Steve said, and the angry look vanished. He smiled thinly and tipped his head. "It had to be your boy, Summers. I left the girl with him. He might act like he's Mr. Perfect, but on the inside he's just as much a freak as everyone else."

"Mark didn't do it," Katie said, and she realized she believed it. "He didn't hurt anyone."

"You sure?" Steve touched his lip, which was puffy and red. Katie wondered if Mark had split it open during their fight at practice that morning. "He seems to like blood. Or maybe it's just my blood he likes."

"I think we're done," Katie said, sick of putting up with Steve's BS. "I have nothing else to say to you."

Steve shrugged and casually stepped aside. "Be my guest," he said, and gestured toward the door.

Katie held her breath as she walked toward him, thinking this was too easy, that Steve had too big an ego to let her just leave like that. And her fears were confirmed when she got to the door and pushed hard on the bar. It wouldn't open. She tried again and again, but it didn't budge.

"It's locked," she said, trying not to panic.

"No shit, Sherlock," he said from behind her.

Katie turned to see him dangling a gold key. Then he flipped it back and forth in his hands.

"We're not done yet." Steve narrowed his eyes at her, giving her a fierce look. "And when we are, you'll be the first to know."

Mark was right. The guy was a total narcissist. He had to be in control. He couldn't take criticism. Katie knew he was a bully on and off the ice. But was he a killer, too?

"Let me out, Steve," she told him, keeping her voice as level as possible, when inside, she was getting scared for real.

"Soon," he replied, and put the key in his pocket. He patted it, grinning like he was having fun playing cat and mouse with her.

"This is ridiculous." Katie reached for the phone in her jacket just as it started to ring. She only had time to see the call was from Mark before Steve closed the gap between them and snatched the phone from her hands.

"Not a good time to talk," he said, and threw it hard across the room.

Katie heard the *crack* as it hit the wall.

Say something, keep talking, distract him, her brain told her. The guy liked to hear his own voice. Maybe she should let him talk until he'd bored himself.

But Katie had had enough.

She grabbed the straps of her book bag with both hands and swung it at him, hitting him hard in the crotch. Then she dropped the bag and took off, racing through the aisles, shoes slapping the floor. If she could just get to the rink, she could find another door, an emergency exit.

She heard Steve cursing, then his footsteps echoing noisily behind her.

"Why are you running from me? I just want to talk," he called out. "I'm not the one who chopped off the girl's hand and gave it to his girlfriend. You should be afraid of Mark."

But Katie kept going, moving through the dark, past row after row of metal lockers. She hit her shin on a bench and bit her lip to stop from crying out.

"I'm not going to hurt you," he said from around the corner. "If you want to leave, you can leave. I won't stop you."

Right, like when she'd tried to leave a minute before?

Katie didn't trust him. She didn't trust her best friend anymore. How could she know that Steve hadn't snuffed Rose? Mark seemed pretty thoroughly convinced that Steve was the killer.

Her shin throbbing, she limped toward a weak light and ended up in the washroom. *Oh, hell,* she realized as she quickly glanced around. It was a dead end. There were no doors or windows in the showers. She felt her way along a tiled wall lined with sinks and mirrors, knowing she was trapped.

She heard Steve's footsteps, getting louder and louder with each breath. And Katie did the only thing she could think to do: she screamed as loudly as she could, hoping a security guard or someone—*anyone*—would hear and get her the hell out of there.

CHAPTER TWENTY-SIX

TESSA

They'd traveled far enough through the tunnels to reach the room below the ice rink where Peter lived. He moved quietly around the space. He lit a candle, then turned around so Tessa could see his face in the flickering glow. Stringy strands of pale hair hung from his scalp where it hadn't burned. He had no eyebrows; those had been singed off in the fire, never to grow back. He wore gray sweatpants and a dark hoodie with a Whitney eagle on the front. The long sleeves hid the scars on his arms. The skin there was thick and ropy, rough like his hands.

In the beginning, it had shocked her, seeing what he'd become—after he'd been in hiding and she'd been in foster care. But it didn't take long for Tessa to embrace her brother again. Now she barely noticed what was different about him. She owed him too much. He had done everything he could to keep her safe.

It was her turn to do the same for him.

Tessa sat on a wooden stool, and Peter came over and crouched at her feet. His body seemed to vibrate even as he went still. He was like an animal, quick and wiry, ready to leap, and far stronger than he appeared.

"I told them what happened that night," she said, "that the girl wasn't breathing, that someone called me from her cell. I told them everything except that it was you on the other end." Tessa squeezed her eyes closed, trying to forget the look on Katie's face when Tessa had accused Mark, trying to forget what Katie had said after.

You're messed up, messed up, messed up.

When all Tessa was doing was trying to spare her brother more pain.

"They took my phone and told me not to leave the dorm until the police checked out everything. But they couldn't stop me from coming here." She reached over to pat the top of his head. "Thank you," she said, "for getting the girl's phone into Mark Summers's locker. They'll have to arrest him now."

Peter grunted, but there was no expression on his face. It was as blank as ever, his blue eyes hard, hiding any pain he'd ever felt before he'd learned not to feel much of anything at all.

He's too damaged and we can't fix him. . . . I'm afraid to be alone with him. . . . He's a danger to us all.

She'd overheard their parents saying that Peter was impossible to love. They hadn't wanted him anymore. They'd packed his things and planned to buy him a one-way plane ticket to Moscow. But when they sat him down and told him their intentions, Peter howled. He didn't want to go. He would never in a million years have gone and left Tessa alone.

We have to send him back; we have no choice.

Peter had decided the very same thing when he'd set the fire: he had no choice.

He didn't realize Tessa would be home. She was supposed to be sleeping over at a friend's house, only the other girl had gotten chicken pox. But when he'd heard his sister screaming, he'd gone inside, even though he'd risked his life to do so.

"You didn't kill Rose," Tessa remarked, and Peter leaned his cheek against her palm. "You just found her, and you dug her a grave in the woods so she could rest in peace. Ashes to ashes, dust to dust, and all that."

Peter made a noise in his throat very much like a cat's purr.

He'd stumbled upon Rose in the old machine room of the headmaster's house. Before he'd taken her lifeless body into the tunnels, he'd used her phone to call Tessa. He thought the dead girl was Katie at first, and he'd been distraught. Tessa had slipped out of Amelia House and found him in the room where he lived. He'd been curled beside the body, making whimpering noises. But Tessa had shown him it wasn't Katie. The girl had a tat. Then Tessa had taken off, wanting to get back to her room before Katie awakened. How was she to know that once she left Peter alone he'd find the bloodred rose on the back of the hand too beautiful to discard? That he would saw the dead girl's hand off and wrap it up like a gift before he took the body to the woods and buried it? Tessa had no idea what was in the package when she'd found it in his room the next morning, before she'd taken off for the trip to the morgue. That was before he'd scrawled Katie's name on the front, tied it with twine, and left it sitting in the rain, on the back steps of the dorm. How could Tessa have imagined he'd put something like that inside, the same way he'd boxed up Mrs. Cottingham's cat and left it on the old lady's porch?

Tessa loved her brother deeply, but she knew he wasn't right.

He never had been.

How could anyone survive undamaged after years in an orphanage without love, without touch, with barely enough food to keep going? His only attachment had been to Tessa. His only loyalty was to his sister. But these past few months, he'd become attached to Katie, too.

When Katie had started dating Mark, Tessa had asked Peter to keep an eye on them. Tessa was afraid that Mark was using her friend, that he was toying with Katie's fragile heart after his breakup with Joelle. And Peter had done it. He had looked after Katie almost too well, to the brink of obsession. Tessa had always known he roamed the tunnels at night. That was how he got everything he needed to live: food and drink from the dorm kitchens or the cafeteria, clothes from locker rooms or lost and founds. But he'd never gone beyond the first floor, and only when it was empty. Until he'd started sneaking upstairs in Amelia House to watch Katie sleep, to bring her a rose from the greenhouse, slipping away before she woke up.

Tessa had caught him at it once, and after that she could hardly sleep for worrying that he'd show up again and leave a rose by Katie's bed. It was a blessing in disguise that Katie's subconscious interpreted those nighttime visits as bad dreams.

Then Peter had started to really get out of control, leaving Katie a rose in the library, lingering in their room so that Tessa had to chase him out . . . and Katie had followed her into the tunnels. Katie had dared to ask if it was Tessa haunting her.

"I don't think Katie trusts me anymore," she told her brother, and he got up from the floor. He began to pace the dimly lit room, his head cocked, his gaze looking above them. "It may be time she learned the whole truth. I have to tell her our secret."

Tessa slipped off the stool as Peter stood quite still, like he heard something she couldn't hear. The way dogs could detect a high-pitched whistle.

"What is it?" she asked.

And then he took off running, leaving Tessa alone in his dungeon-like room, wondering if she'd imagined the faint sound of a scream above her.

CHAPTER TWENTY-SEVEN

KATIE

"Stop yelling!" Steve grabbed Katie by the shoulders, and she tried to wriggle free. "You're not listening to me," he said, and shook her. "I unlocked the door. You can fucking go!"

Steve started to release her and, as his hands fell away, she heard an *oof* and saw him being flung against the wall with the sinks. There was a loud *crack,* and glass shattered, silver rain falling to the tiled floor.

Katie shrieked as Steve crumpled over the sink, his face a bloody mess, the mirror in a million pieces. He moaned loudly, slumping to the floor, and Katie finally saw his attacker fully. He wore old sweats and a black hoodie pulled up around a face so white it looked bloodless. His eyes were the pale blue of ice.

Tessa's eyes, she thought, and blinked. Maybe she was hallucinating.

"Kay-tee."

He came toward her, whispering her name in that strangled way, just like in her dreams.

This wasn't happening. Katie wobbled, her legs unsteady beneath her. "Peter?" she said, and he grunted. He looked like a modern-day Phantom of the Opera, minus the mask, his skin pink and scarred, his hair stringy and sparse.

Oh, God, it was true.

Katie's hands went to her mouth and she swayed. She would have fallen if he hadn't reached out for her.

Peter Lupinski was alive.

She could hear his raspy breathing. Could smell the dank, musky scent of him. And he was touching her.

Katie looked down at the ropy red skin of his hand, and she did something she'd never done in her entire life: she passed out, going down like a rag doll.

"Katie, can you hear me? Please, be okay, *please.*"

Tessa's voice poked at Katie's consciousness. She'd been drifting somewhere between hazy fog and awake since she'd blacked out in the washroom at the ice rink. She could still see Steve's bloody face, which had unnerved her nearly as much as Tessa's brother's cold blue eyes.

No, Katie told herself. It couldn't be Peter Lupinski. Tessa's brother had died ten years ago in the house fire. They'd buried him in the plot with Tessa's parents. Katie had seen the gravesite herself. As far as she knew—outside of fiction—dead people couldn't be resurrected.

"Katie? Please wake up and talk to me."

She heard Tessa's voice, fading in and out for what seemed like hours but was probably minutes. Then she finally cracked open her eyes.

Where was she?

The space was sparsely lit by a candle, and the air smelled like mold and earth and a century's worth of dust. A familiar smell. Was she in a basement? She'd breathed in that messy mix of scents before.

Of course, she realized. The steam tunnels.

Mark had shown her several rooms in the tunnels used to store ancient things. She figured she was in one of those, tucked somewhere under campus.

She struggled to lift her head. She wiggled her fingers but couldn't separate her wrists. Finally, she blinked away the fog, her head pounding, and realized her hands were tied behind her back. What the hell was going on?

"Tessa," she said, her voice hoarse.

"Hey! You're awake!" The old springs in the bare mattress beneath her creaked and Tessa was suddenly beside her. She brushed the hair from Katie's cheeks. "Don't be afraid," she whispered. "You're okay. Peter took care of Steve and brought you here so you'll be safe."

"Then why am I tied up?" She felt like a prisoner, not a guest, in Peter's underground den.

"He's worried that you'll try to leave," Tessa whispered. "He wants to keep you down here with him for a while."

Was she out of her mind?

"Let me go, Tessa," Katie said, shivering.

"Not until you understand." Tessa's face went from relieved to stony. "Not until you listen instead of running off like you did from Dr. Capello's office."

Katie was in an episode of *The Twilight Zone*. She had to be.

She switched her focus from Tessa to the figure that lurked in the shadows behind her roommate. The hood of his black sweatshirt covered most of his head, and the sallow face that peered out seemed almost to disappear like a blank space, like nothing was really there.

"Peter's dead," Katie said, because that was the truth as she'd known it since she'd met Tessa. It was the truth as everyone in Barnard had known it for the past decade.

"No." Tessa shook her head. "He isn't."

"He was buried with your parents," Katie insisted. "Three people died in the fire. *Three.*"

"It wasn't him," Tessa told her, glancing over at the figure in the shadows. "The boy who burned in the house was just some runaway. He didn't belong to anyone. No one missed him."

Just some runaway? No one missed him?

Katie recalled Tessa's words about Rose Tatum when they'd been looking at her Facebook page. *Girls like her ask for trouble. Doesn't it seem like they always end up OD'ing or something?*

So Tessa figured some people were disposable? The way she'd said Rose was disposable to guys like Steve?

Tessa must have detected the revulsion on Katie's face, because she scrambled to explain. "You have to understand.

205

Our parents were about to send Peter back to Russia. They packed up his suitcase. They were taking him to the airport and buying him a ticket. They wanted to put him on a plane like he didn't belong to them anymore. Like he didn't belong to anyone." Tessa looked over at Peter with raw affection on her face. "He didn't want to go. He couldn't leave me. I'm all he has."

Katie could hardly breathe.

Peter Lupinski had set the fire. He'd killed three people, his parents and a boy he barely knew. He had lived and they had perished.

"You knew he did it all along?" Katie asked, tasting bile.

Tessa let out an exasperated sigh. "Don't you get it? He kept me alive. I would have done anything to protect him."

Katie squeezed her eyes shut. *Please, let this not be happening. Let me not be here.* She prayed that when she opened her eyes, she'd be somewhere else. *Anywhere* else.

But when she dared to look again, she was still sitting on an old mattress in a room lit by one candle, and there was Tessa beside her, those familiar clear blue eyes watching her expectantly. Like she was waiting for Katie to say, "Oh, hey! You were just protecting him. Well, then everything's A-OK!"

Katie trembled. "Tessa, untie me *now.*"

But her roommate simply glanced at her brother again, as if he was in charge. As if it was up to him, not her.

Oh, God. Peter wanted to keep her in the tunnels like she was some kind of pet. And Tessa was going to let him?

"Tessa, this is wrong, and you know it."

But Tessa made no move to untie her.

Katie's stomach turned. She pulled as hard as she could against the twine, but it didn't give. *Is it the same twine he'd used on The Box?* she found herself wondering. Was Peter involved in Rose Tatum's death? Was that why Tessa had spun that wild story about Mark calling her?

It was like finally putting together the border to the puzzle when nothing else fit.

"It was him, wasn't it?" Katie said what she was thinking. "He killed Rose, not Mark. Not Steve."

"No!" Tessa jumped up from the mattress. She waved her arms, shaking her head. "Peter didn't kill her. He *found* her. He thought it was you, and he totally freaked out. When he called me from her phone, he was howling like a wounded animal. I'd never heard him in such awful pain, not ever."

Katie stared at Tessa, her stomach cramping. She felt such disgust. "You flat-out lied about Mark. He really was drugged. He didn't do anything."

Tessa's eyes turned rock-hard. "Mark doesn't deserve you. He never did."

"What he doesn't deserve is to spend his life in jail because you helped set him up," Katie said, her chest aching—*everything* aching. How could she have ever trusted Tessa? How could she have believed they were best friends when Tessa had kept so many things from her? Very bad things. Things Katie wished she didn't know, wished she'd never had to hear.

"I had to take care of Peter," Tessa replied without emotion. "I had to take care of *you*. Don't you see?"

Virginia Cottingham had said there was always something off about Peter. And Katie saw clearly for the first time that there was something off about Tessa, too.

"It'll be okay, you'll see," Tessa said, her mouth curving into a thin smile again, one that didn't touch her eyes.

Katie watched as the dark shadow that was Peter moved carefully about the room. He was lighting candles, lots of them. As the room grew a little brighter, and then brighter still, Katie's realized what he meant for her to see: dozens of bloodred roses stuck in old jars and cans. She breathed in their sweet smell, along with the scent of burning wick and wax, and it was all she could do not to gag.

She thought of the rose in the library. The fingers touching her hair. The recurring nightmare that wasn't a nightmare at all.

It had all been Peter, hadn't it?

"For . . . Kay-tee," he rasped, gesturing around him.

Tessa leaned in to whisper, "I think he likes you," as though it were a good thing.

The flickering candles illuminated something else as well: more of Peter's underground home and the things he had collected. Katie's eyes went to several wooden benches and parts of old bleachers that held all kinds of things: books and backpacks, shoes, jackets, purses, ball caps. Things students had lost and he had found? There were dozens of big cans stacked against the wall as well, the kind that bulk fruits and veggies came in, and Katie wondered about the food found down in the basement at Amelia House when Tessa started living there. Was Tessa the one who'd taken it from the dorm's kitchen for Peter? Or did Peter pilfer food for himself?

Then her gaze fell on a collection that made her go cold. Knives of all kinds: penknives, steak knives, several hunting knives, and what looked like a saw. More frightening still, she saw a stun gun, like the ones that the campus cops carried. Did Peter use them to hunt to feed himself? Or did he have plans to use them for something else?

Katie knew then without a doubt that Peter had already done something very bad with the knives or saw. "You cut off Rose's hand, Peter, didn't you?" she said, her voice trembling. "You gave me her hand."

"Roses . . . pretty, yes?" he asked.

Pretty?

Katie tried to stay calm, told herself not to scream. "Sooner or later, they'll know what you've done," she said to him, though his face didn't seem to register that fact. "They'll find something that ties you to Rose. They'll match your fingerprints."

Tessa snorted. "The police will never know anything. Peter doesn't exist in the outside world, and his skin is so scarred he can't leave prints, just smudges."

Katie thought of The Box and the hand, and it came to her, like a light switching on. The thing she'd been trying to sort out in her brain. The police had taken her prints, Tessa's, and the housemother's to rule them out as suspects.

All I can safely tell you is we've taken your prints out of the equation, as well as Miss Lupinski's and Mrs. Gabbert's.

But Tessa had never touched the package that Mrs. Gabbert had brought in from the steps. Tessa's prints shouldn't have even been on it unless she'd handled it before it was received. If only Katie had paid attention.

"I can't stay much longer," Tessa said, glancing at her wristwatch in the candlelight. "They can't realize I've been gone."

"You're not leaving me?" Katie stared at her. How could Tessa even think of taking off without her? "Tessa, this is wrong," Katie said, and tears blurred her vision. "If you're my friend . . . if you love me . . . don't do this."

Tessa walked over and stroked Katie's hair for a moment, and Katie prayed she would change her mind. But instead she leaned over and whispered, "I'll see you in the morning."

Katie moaned. She had to get out. She looked around and found the dark hollow that was the door. If she couldn't use her hands, she'd have to use her legs. Even if she couldn't see in the tunnels, she'd rather take her chances getting lost than spend one minute alone in the dark with Tessa's brother.

Before Tessa left, Katie blurted out, "Wait! I have to pee." The only trick she could think of that might buy her a minute alone.

"Oh." Tessa looked like she hadn't planned on such a thing. "Hold on a sec," she finally said, and got up. She whispered to Peter and he nodded. He went to the far corner of the room and turned around, and Tessa brought an empty tin over. It was big enough to have held about two pounds of peaches. "Can you use this? I'll help."

"I can't pee with you watching," Katie told her. "If you

don't mind, can I just get my hands in front? Then I can do it myself."

Tessa turned her head to look at Peter. He still stood with his back to them. Then she sighed. "All right."

Katie wriggled around on the mattress, sitting on her tied hands and then pulling them around her butt and finally around her bent knees until they were in front of her.

Tessa put the can on the floor.

"Will you turn around, too?" Katie asked.

Tessa didn't appear to like the idea, but she nodded and looked away.

Without wasting another second, Katie took off toward the blackened hollow of the doorway.

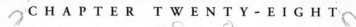
MARK

The door to the men's lockers at the ice rink was unlocked.

Mark pushed his way in and instantly spotted a familiar book bag on the floor. "Katie!" he yelled. "Katie!"

He hurried past the trophy cases and his foot connected with something small. It skidded across the way. He would have let it go, only he had a bad feeling he knew what it was. When he bent over to pick it up, his chest clenched.

He recognized Katie's phone with its pink Hello Kitty cover. Mark pocketed the phone and stood up, heading toward the sinks and showers. "Katie?" he called, trying not to freak out. "Katie, where are you?"

Where the hell were the campus cops? he wondered, and then realized they'd probably pulled a bunch of cars to look for Tessa, who'd vanished from her dorm. Mark knew, though, that they weren't likely to find her unless they went down through the grates, into the tunnels. He was sure that was where she was.

"Katie?" he tried again.

A moan came from the washroom, and Mark rounded the corner to the row of pedestal sinks. He saw the blood first, splashed across a broken mirror and dripping in puddles on the floor.

He let out a held breath when he realized the blood hadn't come from Katie. Its trail led to a man lying on the tiled floor. His face was a bloody mess, but Mark knew it was Steve. What had gone on here? There was no way Katie could have pushed Steve's head into the mirror unless she'd gotten superpowers.

"Getty," he said, and nudged him with his foot. "Are you alive?"

"I guess so," Steve muttered.

"Where's Katie?" Mark asked. "If you hurt her, I'll kill you, I swear," he added. "Only it looks like someone else tried to do that already."

"I didn't do anything," Steve whispered through his bloodied mouth, and struggled to sit up, leaning against the tiled wall. "The guy came out of nowhere."

"Who?"

"He was so fucking strong."

"*Who?*" Mark asked again.

"I don't know," Steve said, touching his face and wincing. "He came from behind. I didn't see who it was. I was out cold for a few, and when I woke up, she was gone."

"How'd you get her to come here?"

"A chick will do anything for her BFF, right?"

"You pretended to be Tessa?" Mark asked. "How'd you know Katie wasn't with her in the dorm?"

Steve shrugged. He was too busy inspecting his injuries.

Mark could have kicked the guy for doing something so cruel. Yes, Katie would do just about anything for Tessa. Only Tessa wasn't on the up-and-up these days any more than Steve. Mark couldn't figure who the mystery man was who'd beaten up Getty and taken Katie, but he was sure Tessa knew who it was. And his gut told him Katie was with Tessa.

"Christ, I think I swallowed some teeth," Steve mumbled as he fingered his mouth. "Help me up, would you?"

"Help you? Like you helped me the night of the party? Sure," Mark said, and pulled out his cell, calling his dad and telling him, "If you want Rose's killer, he's lying in a pool of his own blood in the ice rink showers. And, no, I didn't do it. Someone else did, and now Katie's missing."

He hung up.

"Where you going, man?" Steve called after him as Mark walked toward the machine room behind the showers.

There was a grate leading into the tunnels behind a bunch of oversized water heaters. He found the grille already loosened and shoved it aside. He had no idea who'd taken Katie or where they'd gone. But if Tessa had disappeared, he knew she was underground. It could take him all night to cover just one section of the tunnels. Scouring every passage could take days, and he didn't have days.

Mark moved through the tunnels, feeling his way along

the damp stone at his sides. He paused for a second in the dark, every nerve in his body suddenly on fire. Was he crazy or could he hear voices and the scuff of someone's footsteps coming toward him?

"Katie?" he yelled, hoping she could hear.

She was near, he knew, his pulse thumping. He kept on a straight path, the footsteps getting louder. His eyes didn't have time to adjust, so he could rely only on his ears and his fingers.

"Katie!" he tried again. "Katie!"

And then he heard her cry out, "Mark!"

"Keep coming," he told her. "I'm close."

He kept saying her name so she could follow his voice through the dark. He moved toward her as fast as he could until she plowed into him headfirst. He wrapped his arms around her, pressing his face into her hair, breathing in the scent of her.

"We've got to get out of here," Katie wailed, shaking uncontrollably. "Tessa's been helping him. He's not dead after all—"

"Who?" he asked as he tried to untie her hands.

"Please, let's go," she said, tugging her bound wrists away, her voice trembling as much as the rest of her. "He's right behind me."

As soon as the words were out of her mouth, Mark felt someone grab his shoulders, pulling him down. He heard a guttural growl as hands rough as sandpaper wrapped around his neck so tightly all he could do was gasp.

Mark couldn't breathe. The hands closed in on his windpipe, cutting off air. He reached behind him, grabbed for flesh or eyes and tried to claw and scratch. There was barely room to move, hardly a chance to fight back.

"Peter, no!" Katie was yelling. "Peter, stop!"

Mark was choking, his consciousness turning as dark as the tunnel around him. His arms fell to his sides and he slumped to his knees, his palms on the stone as he slowly slid to the ground. He didn't see his life flash before him, but he did see flashes in the dark, tiny bursts of lightning. He felt the tail end of an electrical jolt, and then the hands slipped off his throat and he fell back, gasping and sucking in oxygen like a drunk chugging liquor.

He heard a thud as someone hit the stone floor, and the noise of legs and arms slapping the rock in convulsions.

"Mark!" Katie sobbed his name. "Say that you're okay!"

"I'm . . . okay," he breathed, rolling onto his back, gulping in musty air. He felt Katie's hands touch his face, the twine around her wrists scratching his cheek.

And somewhere very near, Mark heard Tessa say over and over, "I'm sorry, I'm sorry, I'm so sorry."

Mark felt Katie's head turn, and she asked in a shaky voice, "Tessa, you stunned Peter, not Mark?" Then she was crying. "You did that for me," she said, sobbing. "You did the right thing."

"I had no choice," Tessa replied in an eerily calm voice. "I lied to you, Katie. He wanted to keep you down here. He wasn't going to let you go. I couldn't let him do that, could I?"

"No," Katie said. "No." She wrapped her arms around Mark and held on to him tightly. "Don't let me go," she whispered.

"I won't," he told her. "I swear to God, I won't."

CHAPTER TWENTY-NINE

TESSA

Dear Katie,

If I said I'm sorry a million times, it wouldn't be enough. If I said I love you, it would mean nothing because of the lies and the secrets I kept. But I am sorry and I do love you. I would do anything for you, and I think I proved that. Maybe someday, you'll forgive me and want to be friends again. I hope you understand that I had to do all I could to save Peter, even if he was too broken to fix. I had to try, and if I had to do it again, I would. Does that make me a very bad person or a very good one?

Yours always,
Tessa

CHAPTER THIRTY

KATIE

The sun shone down brightly, as if nothing in the world were out of place and this day were like every other spring day before it.

But Katie knew good and well that it wasn't.

Rose Marie Tatum had been buried a half hour earlier. And she'd been wearing the St. Sebastian medallion, the one the police had found around her neck in that shallow grave in the woods. Katie had given it to Mark to protect him. Since Rose hadn't had anyone to protect her in this life, Katie hoped maybe St. Sebastian would protect her in the afterlife. It was worth a shot.

Dozens of students from Whitney had attended the service and the school had paid for Rose's burial, along with the huge spray of red roses that covered her casket. Katie was glad for the turnout since she didn't see anyone show up who acted like Rose's family. A number of townsfolk had paid their respects, too, and the other waitress from the diner who had been Rose's roommate. Katie heard that Rose's mother had always been fonder of alcohol than she was of her own child, and no one had ever really been sure who her father was.

In a way, Rose had been as much an orphan as Tessa.

They'd both experienced plenty of pain way too early in life.

The police ruled Rose's death an overdose and charged Steve Getty with manslaughter. Only Steve had disappeared from the school's clinic in the middle of the night—twelve fresh stitches in his face—before the Barnard police could arrest him. Word had it that his ambassador father had swooped in and jetted off with him, taking him out of the country this time, most likely to a place where he couldn't be extradited.

Slimy bastard, Joelle had texted Katie when everyone learned what Steve had done and that he'd skipped town. Now he got away with murder.

On the other hand, Peter Lupinski wasn't getting away with anything, not this time around. He'd survived getting Tasered but faced three counts of murder in the first degree. Peter Mikhail Lupinski—the *real* Peter—would likely be locked up for the rest of his life. Cutting off a dead girl's hand was the least of it. Dr. Capello wanted him committed to a psychiatric facility rather than the state prison. She was quoted in the *Barnard Gazette* as saying, "He's severely physically and emotionally scarred. He isn't fit to stand trial."

In that same article, Katie read that they'd be digging up

the bones from Peter Lupinski's grave. Dr. Arnold and his associates at the hospital's cadaver lab would consult with a forensic anthropologist to try to determine who had really died in the fire instead of Peter.

"He didn't belong to anyone. No one missed him," Tessa had said so dismissively. But Katie knew she was wrong.

Everyone belonged to *someone*. Everyone came from somewhere. Everyone had a name and a right to be properly put to rest.

How had Katie not guessed that her best friend was hiding something so big, so dark? Tessa had kept the secret well. Had guarded it fiercely. All to protect a brother too damaged to lead a normal life.

And Tessa had been damaged, too. According to the *Gazette,* the local prosecutor was still trying to decide what charges to press against her. Katie hoped Dr. Capello would help Tessa get treatment, too. Maybe she wasn't too broken to be fixed.

No matter what Tessa had done, Katie felt incredibly sorry for her. She'd hardly had a chance to be anything but broken.

How she wished things had been different! If only Tessa had opened up to her, had let her help. In a way, Katie felt like she'd buried her best friend today, too.

And it sucked.

"Time to go," Mark said, and tugged her hand as the crowd of mourners began to disperse.

Katie looked away from Rose's grave and into Mark's face. His neck was still mottled with bruises from Peter's hands.

But his eyes were calm, and she knew he was relieved to have the truth come out despite the rough path to get there.

"Do you believe in heaven?" she asked on a whim, thinking of her father and her grandfather. Of Rose Tatum and the Lupinskis. Surely they were in a better place.

"I guess I do," Mark said, and glanced above them at the endless blue sky. Then he looked at her so warmly her heart melted. "If you don't believe in something, you've got nothing, right?"

"Right." Katie squeezed his hand and smiled.

EPILOGUE

The ice rink was packed.

Katie figured every Whitney Prep student was there, filling the stands, eager to cheer on what was left of their hockey squad. It wasn't the state championship, which they'd had to forfeit because of all the turmoil. But the Briarcliff Bears, state champions by default, wanted to play the Soaring Eagles nonetheless, and the Eagles had accepted.

Everyone on campus was stoked. It was something fun and light after weeks that had seemed so dark and harsh.

"It's just a friendly match, nothing at stake," Mark had told Katie when she'd talked to him before he'd gone into the locker room to gear up.

But Katie knew it was way more than that.

This was Mark's last game as a senior, his last game as captain, and he wanted to win. With Steve Getty gone to God knows where and Charlie a scratch while he recovered, the team wasn't at full strength. But Mark had something to prove. If anyone could lead them to a win by guts alone, Katie was sure it was him.

It felt odd, at first, sitting in the stands without Tessa attached to her hip. But Katie knew Tessa was attending daily counseling sessions and trying to get her life back together after losing her scholarship and being expelled from Whitney. She was being held at a juvie detention center the next town over until the judge presiding over her case decided how to proceed. Katie had already gotten a letter from Tessa, apologizing for everything. She planned to write her back one of these days. Just not yet. Soon. When she knew better what to say.

"Hey, move the ugly hobo, would you?" Joelle Needham scowled down at her from the aisle. "You're taking up two seats with that thing."

Katie murmured, "Sorry," before putting her bag between her feet.

"That's better." Joelle wiggled her curvy backside into the space beside Katie and shoved a bag of popcorn into her hands. "Eat up, Barton," she said, before drawing out a compact and touching up her lip gloss. "You're looking scary scrawny these days. I swear, you wouldn't even have matching socks if I didn't keep an eye on you."

Katie suppressed a giggle. That Joelle had decided to shuck her posh friends and start hanging around her was downright funny.

She started stuffing her face with popcorn, then mumbled with her mouth full, "Are you happy now?"

Joelle gave her a sideways look and sighed. "I swear, you're like a new puppy. Am I going to have to paper-train you?"

Katie almost choked on a kernel laughing.

She stopped goofing off when the lights went down and a spotlight appeared, shining on the open slot in the boards where the home team would come skating out.

The crowd began to roar as the announcer wailed, "Your Soaring Eagles starting lineup!"

Katie held her breath until she saw Mark appear, a huge smile on his face like she hadn't seen in weeks.

"And introducing the captain, Mark Suuuuummers," the announcer said, dragging out the name like he'd never stop.

Katie's heart felt near to bursting. She couldn't help it. She jumped to her feet, clapping and hooting, showering Joelle with popcorn.

"For God's sake," Joelle muttered, brushing the buttery stuff from her lap. "You're not just a puppy, you're a puppy on crack. I think being your friend is going to take some getting used to."

But Katie was screaming "*Gooo*, Eagles!" so loudly she couldn't hear much of anything except the sound of her own voice.

She realized something in that moment: it didn't matter that this game didn't count and Mark wouldn't get the state championship MVP award to add to Whitney's trophy case. Maybe it wasn't the picture-perfect ending to their senior year that either of them had dreamed of. But considering what they'd been through, it wasn't half bad. No, it wasn't bad at all.

ACKNOWLEDGMENTS

Many thanks to Wendy Loggia and Krista Vitola for their insightful and meticulous notes during the creative process. *Very Bad Things* would not be the roller-coaster ride that it is without such brilliant direction. Big hugs to Christina Hogrebe for all her hard work behind the scenes. And much love to my husband, my daughter, Grandma, and Nana, who gave me time to write (and kept me sane throughout!).

ABOUT THE AUTHOR

SUSAN MCBRIDE is the award-winning author of fiction for adults and teens. She lives in a suburb of St. Louis with her husband, their daughter, and two cats who think they're dogs. You can visit her at SusanMcBride.com and on Facebook at SusanMcBrideBooks.